Nonsensically Challenged

Volume 1

DEDICATION

In memory of Daisy Garland.

At the tender age of six, Daisy Garland died in her sleep. She suffered from epilepsy and died of SUDEP (sudden unexpected death in epilepsy patients). Daisy bore her illness with great dignity and courage; always smiley, kind and loving, she left a strong impression on everyone who met her. Her memory lives on in the charity set up in her name. The charity helps other little ones like Daisy whose lives are blighted by drug-resistant epilepsy.

Lesley Truchet & Chris Fielden

INTRODUCTION 1

by Lesley Truchet

I was introduced to the prestigious Mr Christopher Fielden when scanning the net one day. I came across his annual humorous short story competition, To Hull & Back, and duly submitted an entry in 2015 and again in 2016.

From then on I have received regular newsletters from Chris. One of them mentioned an upcoming challenge organised by Chris and Mike Scott Thompson, 'Mike's Not-Entirely-Serious Wantonly-Rule-Breaking Adverb Writing Challenge'. The words 'rule breaking' piqued my interest. I always feel deliciously naughty cocking a snoot at regulations. I wrote and submitted a couple of adverb filled stories for the challenge. It was during the process of writing these adverbially rule-breaking masterpieces that I thought to myself, *Wouldn't it be a good idea to introduce a similar challenge but with nonsensical stories?* I emailed my idea to Chris and expected a response saying something like, 'Thanks, I'll keep it in mind.'

Although I don't remember the actual wording, the response I received from Chris was something to this effect: 'Great idea, Lesley. Are you up for organising it with me?' I remember thinking, unlike being asked to sleep with Prince Phillip, (a great honour but I wouldn't really want to do it,) this was a great honour, and I really wanted to do it. I sent a big YES to Chris and not long afterward I gave birth to the title of 'Lesley's Nifty Nib-Nibbling Nonsensical Narrative Writing Challenge' (Prince Phillip had nothing to do with the conception).

Thanks to Chris's big-hearted benevolence, this

challenge supports a UK family run charity which helps children with drug resistant epilepsy. More details about the charity are mentioned elsewhere in this book.

Creative writing allows the writer to express his or her ideas in the course of a story. However, most genres follow certain rules. A love story is expected to end happily, a crime should be solved etc.

Nonsense writing is almost like another rule-breaking exercise. There is no need to worry about logic. A writer can create the most bizarre protagonists, have them performing absurd and totally improbable feats in preternatural settings, creating a scenario beyond the barriers of our awareness. The challenge of penning a nonsense story stretches a writer's imagination to its limits – and beyond.

In the following pages, there are 100 well-presented and very diverse nonsensical stories for you to enjoy.

Sink comfortably into your favourite armchair with a glass of red, or a cuppa, forget your cares and take a stroll into nonsense land. Be careful, who knows what may happen in there.

INTRODUCTION 2

by Chris Fielden

Welcome to the first nonsense challenge anthology. Being a writer of fantasy and a huge fan of authors with amazing imaginations, like David Gemmell, Douglas Adams, Philip K. Dick, Roald Dahl, Robert E. Howard, Stephen King, Terry Pratchett, Ursula K. Le Guin – I'll stop there, as this list is in danger of becoming epic – it's a huge pleasure to present this fantabulous collection of 100 nonsensical yet wonderfully inventive, fantastical stories.

Lesley's Nifty Nib-Nibbling Nonsensical Narrative Writing Challenge was launched in November 2016. We received our 100th submission at the beginning of March 2017. At the time of writing, we've already received a plethora of stories for the second anthology.

The nonsense challenge raises awareness of the importance of a coherent plot and a gratifying story conclusion. Many new writers fail to end stories in a way that's satisfying for the reader. This challenge highlights that common mistake.

One of the things I enjoy about running the challenges are the conversations I have with authors after they've submitted. While running the nonsense challenge, I enjoyed some interesting email correspondence with Canadian author, Olivier Breuleux.

As some of you may know, I dislike the use of exclamation marks in stories. This is probably because they're often overused and/or misused, particularly in humorous writing. Through running the To Hull & Back short story competition, I read around 1,000,000 words of humorous tales each year. By doing that, I see an excessive amount of unnecessary and incorrectly used exclamation points. This is, at least in part, why I delete them all.

That said, this book does contain a story that contains exclamation marks. The author, Helen Combe, was deviously clever and left me no option but to leave them in. You will see why when you read her story. I'm envious of her cunning…

The conversation I had with Olivier thoroughly explored the use of exclamation marks from both the reader's and publisher's point of view. It was so interesting that I published the discussion as a post on my blog. You can read it here:

www.christopherfielden.com/short-story-tips-and-writing-advice/exclamation-marks.php

I've also discussed apostrophes, point of view errors, consistent formatting, spellings and many other aspects of writing with different writers. I look forward to any correspondence that may occur in the future.

There are lots of new writing challenges in the pipeline and many others already running on my website. You can learn about them all here:

www.christopherfielden.com/writing-challenges/

The long-term aim is to develop a writing community that contributors can feel proud to be associated with. I'm hoping that together we'll raise thousands of pounds for worthy causes over the coming years.

The only other thing to mention is that the stories in this book are presented in the order they were received. Where supplied, the writer's biography appears with their story.

Over and out.

INTRODUCTION 3

by The Daisy Garland

Set up 12 years ago after the death of our then only daughter, Daisy, who died of SUDEP (sudden unexpected death in epilepsy patients) at the age of six, The Daisy Garland charity works exclusively for children with drug-resistant epilepsy; there are 18,000 in the UK who suffer from this life-shortening illness. We help by funding specialist Ketogenic dietitians who work in NHS hospitals countrywide. The Ketogenic diet is a NICE recommended treatment for drug-resistant epilepsy. As well as being the leading charity providing funding for Ketogenic dietitians, we also provide grants for night-time breathing and SATs monitors, keeping children safe while they sleep and reducing the risk of SUDEP.

We are extremely grateful to the contributors and editors of this anthology for their kind and generous support. And to you for buying this book. Your donation will make a positive difference to the life of a child with drug-resistant epilepsy.

Thank you.

ACKNOWLEDGMENTS

Big thanks to Lesley Truchet for conceiving and helping me bring the Nonsense Challenge to life. You can learn more about Lesley here:
www.facebook.com/lesley.truchet

Thanks to David Fielden for designing the cover of this book and building and maintaining my website. Without him, I'd never have created a platform that allowed the writing challenges I run to be so successful. You can learn more about Dave's website building skills at:
www.bluetree.co.uk

Finally, a suitably nonsensically-worded HUGEMONGOTASTIC thank you to everyone who has submitted stories and supported this crazy idea and, in turn, the Daisy Garland charity. At the time of writing, we are already well on the way to 100 stories for *Nonsensically Challenged Volume 2*. Without the support of all the writers who submit their stories, this simply wouldn't be possible.

1: THE INSENSITIVE SLORRT

by Lesley Truchet

"Have you seen that, Tinkers?" The hamplah chick pointed its beak.

"Oh no, they're a protected species." The spirlite observed a young slorrt brutally slashing at some delicate puffia blooms, scattering their ruined purple petals.

"Pity you're such a good spirlite, or you could turn him into a warty wereprod," said the hamplah.

"I'm not one of those witless wand-swishers," Tinkers snorted. "But I can be very bad when it suits me. Leave this to me." She flew off after the departing slorrt.

Later that evening the young slorrt woke up screaming.

"I dreamt that I was in a field of giant puffias," the slorrt sobbed between his words whilst his mother comforted him. "One of them trapped my head inside its bell shaped petals and squeezed. I couldn't breathe. Everything went black. I was dying and I could hear them sniggering." The slorrt whimpered and shuddered in distress.

Eventually he calmed down and closed his eyes, and therefore didn't notice a tittering, miniscule creature flying over his bed and out of the window. Afterwards, his dream re-occurred frequently, reminding him to treat puffias and all other living things with more respect.

~

1

Lesley Truchet's Biography

Lesley Truchet has been writing for several years and has a number of short stories, articles and poems published on paper and on the internet. She is currently writing her first novel.

2: NECROMANTIC COBBLERS

by Christopher Fielden

"And lo, the fiery wolfen-hippo shall rise from the ashes of destruction," said Grandiloquence, the mage.

And lo, it did. The fiery wolfen-hippo looked down upon herself. She was indeed a hippo that was wolfen. And fiery.

"You said I'd be reborn a phoenix."

"Glorious," said Grandiloquence. "You shall be known as Bombast."

"I shall not," said Bombast. "Turn me into a phoenix. Now."

"The monk doth know his dangleberry and they are molten."

"Eh?"

"The flatulence of forecast is wantonly chanking, ocelot and glabella."

"Not this again, Grandiloquence; talking cobblers, pretending madness made you cock up the incantation..."

"You ask my foot, yet taste my wilson?" Grandiloquence raised an eyebrow. "Sweet child of pubes, may your chasm be burnished."

Bombast, the fiery wolfen-hippo, took a threatening step towards Grandiloquence. "One more drivel-laden sentence and you'll suffer my wrath."

Grandiloquence laughed. "Collywobbles cannot smite me, Bombast. The sky hums with udders and protects–"

Bombast breathed fire. Grandiloquence burned.

"And lo, the watery water-melon shall rise from the ashes of destruction," said Bombast.

And lo, it did. The watery water-melon looked down upon himself. He was indeed a water melon. And watery.

"Have some of that, you lunatic," said Bombast.

~

Christopher Fielden's Biography

Chris writes, runs a humorous short story competition, plays drums and rides his motorcycle, sometimes to Hull. And back again.

He has recently started running writing challenges and hopes to publish 1,000s of authors in the support of charity.

www.christopherfielden.com

3: WRONG STONES

by S.B. Borgersen

"I can only obble," she bibbled, "all I see are buffoons of macaroons."

"Not me," he blankied, "my nail files have floated down the strawberry tarts."

And so the two blew all the bowls off the chairs and knelt on the waves of linoleum, counting the starry sky beneath their feet.

When they both reached minus 18 in sync, he said to her, "Get your apple out girlie-pie, we are going up into the peach stone."

And with that they trowelled their way down through the linoleum to the floor above, where the merino cherries were sitting, counting, backwards, the bowls on the chairs.

"Wrong stones," he said, "we need to keep flibbering higher."

And so they trowelled through the lightning until their nibbles bled ice-cream and the wallpaper joined in the fun.

~

S.B. Borgersen's Biography

Originally from England, Sue's home is Nova Scotia where she creates art, fiction, poetry and music, thanks to her patient husband, their boisterous dogs and an ever-growing collection of weird instruments.

www.sueborgersen.com

4: OUT OF HOUSTON

by Marie Rennard

"Houston, I think we're having a problem,
    "the whale has swum away from the mother planet,
    "she's put the tyres of the bike around her neck to avoid getting drowned.
    "Send us a red herring,
    "and a lot of peanuts,
    "the whale has swum away with the sun on her tail."
    "Houston here: why do you need peanuts?
    "And what is this 'we've tried sawing white stones'?"
    "Houston, please stop asking silly questions,
    "if you don't have peanuts, send chickpeas.
    "Use fast mail, this is an emergency case, Houston,
    "we're in the whale.
    "The more distance it makes, the more it shrinks,
    "and the less room we've got to store peas."
    "Will you stop arguing?"

~

Marie Rennard's Biography

Marie Rennard is a French translator and a teacher.

5: MILKING THE BILLY

by Simon Russell

At a quarter to ten I picked up the pen to write that I had something to do at a quarter to two.

At a quarter to twelve I read the note to see what I had to do at a quarter to two.

The note said 'milk for tea'.

"Milk for tea," said I to me, "I never take milk in tea, so what did I have to do at quarter to two?"

At a quarter to four there was a bang on the door and a red faced man stood there.

Said he to me, "Did you forget you were coming to tea at a quarter to three and now it's a quarter to four?"

Said I to him, "I made the note that I had something to do at quarter to two but could not remember what to do."

Said he to me, "You had to milk the goat at quarter to two to be with me at quarter to three for tea."

"Argh," said me to he, "I could not milk the goat at a quarter to two as she is a him."

~

Simon Russell's Biography

No author biography supplied.

6: FOOD FOR THOUGHT

by Michael Rumsey

This is a not very highly classified transcript of a recorded meeting held in the PM's office and picked up on short wave radio.

The Source: Estimated to be somewhere up there, several worm holes and mega-parsecs North East of Botswana.

The Time: Once upon a.

"Sit, Semolina. Some surprising spectacular sensational scene seen so Soya says?"

"Verily, Prime Macarone."

"And where did my two favourite expeditionary exploratoroians encounter this episode?"

"Earth, Excellency."

"Erth?"

"Earth, sir. There's an a in it."

"Did you say a?"

"Aye."

"What sort of a?"

"A capital A."

"Alphacumomega astounding. And how did you uncover this promising peculiar phenomenon?"

"By keeping my nose close to the ground, sir, rather like the creature itself."

"By all the chopsticks and digit bowls, a palatable event to be sniffed at then. I have never known you to be tongue twisted so verbally verify. What exactly did your visual apertures behold?"

"An alert, ambitious and avaricious Aardvark airily ambling along an adventurous African avenue, aware that abundant and appetising anthills awaited arrival."

"Well batter my blueberries, Semmy my sweet, quite a mouthful. I think this is a recipe that could cook up sustenance for contemplation."

~

Michael Rumsey's Biography

Michael lives in Athens with wife Maria, dog Sammy, several Greek Tax Demands and a laptop that just occasionally does as it is told.

7: DONALD'S IN CHARGE NOW

by R E Nots

As the door closed, the elephants came out of their holes. Hibernation had finished three days ago and the chance to come out into the daylight excited them. Much anticipation surrounded this special day, as it would see many younger elephants fly off in search of a new home.

Donald, with his gleaming bright green tusks, was tasked with ensuring the exodus was a success.

He'd spent the previous three days constructing the launch ramp and his nervousness was evident.

The 20 elephants lined up before the ramp, behind the tape line. Donald was proud of how straight the line was.

"RUN AND FLAP," Donald trumpeted, as was the customary flight command.

With all their might the elephants ran and flapped past the line, up over the take off ramp and flew.

Reaching above the height of the windowsill, the sun hurting their eyes, the young elephants could see the city stretching out before them, their hearts beating in time with their miniscule wings.

They headed for their freedom.

THUMP... The window wasn't open. The pink elephants hit and slid down the glass and landed unceremoniously next to a potted cactus...

Dishevelled Donald shook his head in dismay.

~

R E Nots' Biography

Me writing something... preposterous... However, Mr Fielden can often be annoying enough to make things happen, so with a slightly political theme this nonsensical short story was born. Two wrongs don't make a writer... or something like that.

8: ANIMOSPODDITY FOR BEGINNERS

by John Notley

While pursuing my normal Sunday activity of animospoddity (observation of unusual species of animal) I was lucky enough to find the one which had eluded me for years – the Lesser-Spotted Welliphant.

Walking through the paddy fields of Ireland, his natural habitat, I came upon this magnificent creature. The Welliphant is easily recognised by its broad back, stumpy legs encased in wellies and the ever present bowler hat. It is advisable not to approach too close as the Welliphant is quite shy. Although he generally stays within his own territory, he has been known to wander further afield. So if the animal should ask his way home, do not shout else he will flap his ears and gently float away.

My next mission is to locate a Flat-Footed Platypuss, native to Australia, where they are fondly known as Shelaghs. These unique animals are a hybrid species; part duck, part beaver and the rest pussycat. This versatile creature is thus able to fish, burrow and catch mice often, all at the same time.

My next book will feature the Long-Necked Peruvian Plum Plucker, often mistaken for a One-Horn Purple People Eater which, as everyone knows, does not exist.

~

John Notley's Biography

John, a retired travel agent, having failed to make his

fortune, has taken up his pen again, hoping to redress the situation. He had a few stories and poems published some years ago but feels it's time to hit the jackpot.

linkedin.com/in/john-notley-503666102/

9: ROCKS IN HIS HEAD

by Glen Donaldson

Only a madman would draw scissors three times in a row, thought Miles Munro, four times World Rock Paper Scissors champion, as he again tried to predict what his four-fingered opponent, Birch Prendergast, would do next.

A prodigiously-gifted 'blitz' player who'd established his psychological bona fides by studying game theory, Miles sensed his mild-mannered adversary didn't really like being around people at all, excepting this once a year opportunity to showcase his prodigious brand of finger-dazzle.

Known in tournament circles as Masterchief Munro, Miles was a practised hand, so to speak, in the black arts of competitive mind-games: attempting to double-think and psyche out challengers while all the time clawing for advantage using pattern recognition, body language analysis and the finer points of the old mentalist trick 'Sicilian Reasoning'. Heck, when it came right down to it, Miles wasn't above even trash-talking his foes to throw them off balance.

Yet amidst this great hall of mirrors, Miles himself made the transparently rookie error of tucking the tip of his thumb into the crook of his index finger, telegraphing an obvious rock. It was over, and his career on the pro touring circuit had likewise just hit rock bottom.

~

Glen Donaldson's Biography

Glen Donaldson avoids clichés like the plague and admits to being disappointed that a group of squid is not called a squad.

www.goosefleshsite.wordpress.com

10: NUTS AND DOLTS

by Braid Anderson

Once upon a time, Lunatic – he's an insect from the moon – went to the doctor with a head under his lump.

"What happened?" asked Dr Pyramid.

"I was putting on some toilet water and the seat fell down."

Dr Pyramid gave him an obscene prescription. Lunatic, being prone to premature articulation, called the doctor a pyramidiot. Dr Pyramid then sued Lunatic for definition of character.

On his way to court, the doctor met a colleague, Doctor Psycho.

"Hello," said Pyramid.

Wonder what he meant by that? thought Psycho.

Dr Pyramid's lawyer explained to the court that the good doctor was viewed as a 'real asset' by his fellow practitioners.

"Only two letters too many," muttered Judge Godly.

"That's it, I'm off," said Pyramid.

"Couldn't have put it better myself," said the judge, whose brother was an Anglican bishop. HE proposed to his bride by singing 'Abide With Me' out of tune.

Judge Godly had just finished reading a collection of articles written for the *Rome Herald* by Vice Versa (who also wrote erotic poems), entitled 'The Secret Acts of the Apostles'. His next case was an action by the RSPCA against a Mr Miserly Hillfarmer, whose defence was 'The Lord is my Shepherd'.

~

Braid Anderson's Biography

No author biography supplied.

11: MURDERER AT LARGE

by Ville Nummenpää

I was walking along the road with my mentally disturbed and ugly wife, when we saw him – Brubaker. The murderer had strangled the entire city council of Stronghamfordshire just a few weeks prior.

He was firing his pistol at us in a reckless manner. Several of the bullets hit my brain, but luckily the gun was just a 22-caliber. Painful, but not fatal. My wife also took several hits to her face, but she was so ugly that the gunshot wounds actually improved her looks. Miraculously, the bullets also cured her schizophrenia.

Fortunately, a large concert piano landed on Brubaker at that very minute. Otherwise he might have continued firing, and possibly killed us.

The police arrived soon after and the whole episode was resolved. Oh, how we laughed.

Brubaker is now serving a three month sentence at a minimum security prison and we visit him every Christmas, bringing him cakes and soft drinks.

My wife and I are now happier than ever. Which is not to say happy, just happier.

~

Ville Nummenpää's Biography

Ville just won a prestigious stage play-award in his home country Finland, and is launching a new career writing for television, possibly cinema.

He's always up for writing something fun, for any

excuse imaginable.

12: THE NOT-TO-BE STOREE OF EDWINA BUNKUM-DROLLE

by Katy Wimhurst

"Hello. Hello. I'm a storee looking for an author," said the storee to the author. "My storee is about Edwina Bunkum-Drolle, a 39-year-old nomaddic woman from Lincoln, who, seeking to be an artist who can interpret evereething, including the sunlit dust of realitee, goes in search of the bumhole of the world (12 miles from Coventry), climbs an invisible mountain near Cambridge to speak to a techno-druid about hippy nonsense, accidentallee averts an apocalypse in Ipswich, has her ideas temporarilee sukked out by an evil vaccuum cleaner at Northampton universitee, but then, one day while gazing at the unwinding tressses of the setting sun, decides too return to Lincoln, where she forms an earth commune with an indigenous taxii driver who makes raather good cups of jaffa-cake tea."

The author contemplated the storee with disdain. "Leaving aside your obvious problems with spelling and punctuation, unrealistic characters, clunky prose and very odd plot," he said, running a finger over his copy of Dostoevsky's *The Idiot*. "It's clear that this is a ridiculous story which makes little sense. You're not taking writing seriously. Writing is a serious job for serious people. So go away."

So the storee went away.

~

Katy Wimhurst's Biography

Katy Wimhurst writes fiction and non-fiction and has been published in various magazines and anthologies, including *The Puritan*, The Short Story, Black Pear Press, Fabula Press, the guardian.com, *Breath and Shadow*, and *Bust Down the Doors and Eat All the Chickens*.

13: DIPSTICKS AND FIZGIGS

by Susan Powis

"Blundergrast. My dipstick. Today I shall go to winkel at my people. And I shall travel in Black Mary."

"Your Pomposity," Blungergrast bowed, his dingle touching his katz as he handed over the dipstick. "You may need more than the dipstick if you travel in Black Mary for she is most underwhelming."

"I shall not go in the Royal Cucina for a casual winkel. It is far too... what is the word?"

"Golden, Your Bombosity?"

"Quite so. And too cramped. My fizgig would get squashed. Black Mary it is. Send word."

"As Your Flatuosity commands." Blundergrast hurried off.

The winkel was a huge disappointment. The dipstick was ignored. The people barely observed the huge fizgig poking out of the window.

"Perhaps the Cucina was a better idea," His Girthness proclaimed sadly. "Those stupid people did not even know who I was, though I waved the dipstick most regally and stuck out my most wonderful fizgig, which actually blew off as we rounded the corner by the Royal Hamptons."

"It is fortuitous, Your Baldness, that one of the courtiers picked it up."

"And I shall order another dipstick. No one dips to this bejewelled stick."

~

Susan Powis's Biography

Sue Powis, from Birmingham, formerly a Special Needs Teacher and Speech Therapy Assistant. Retired and having the most fun a person can have on their own (thanks TP), apart from jumping up and down in muddy puddles with my granddaughter.

14: BOOGERS ARE LIKE BRUSSELS SPROUTS

by C.L. Verhagen

Boogers are like Brussels sprouts,
sometimes they're green and sometimes they're brown,
sometimes they're oblong and sometimes they're round.

Sometimes they're goopy,
and they smell really bad.
Sometimes if you eat them,
you gag just a tad.

You can throw them like baseballs,
or they can be flicked,
If you hide them under chairs,
sometimes they'll stick.

Not everyone knows where they come from, it's true,
but I think boogers are like Brussels sprouts, don't you?

~

C.L. Verhagen's Biography

No author biography supplied.

15: CHEERS MUM, CHEERS CHRIS

by Martin Strike

Weekday tea-times are in ruins. One can rarely condone celebrity stalking, but really, Mum – Chris from *Eggheads*?

"Who will beat the Eggheads?"

Well it won't be you, Mum, not in the next 18-months, anyway. The real victim in this is me. They took BBC2 away from our tele as part of your restraining order, so your incarceration condemns me to a year and a half of *Tipping* bloody *Point* while eating peanut-butter sandwiches as the cooking programmes don't start 'til eight (you can't count *Come Dine With Me* as you would kill me if I had strangers round). I'll miss you of course, but not as much as I will Jeremy Vine. And Daphne.

The magistrate wouldn't accept your explanation that it was Chris's glasses you couldn't resist. He had a point, reminding you that the last celebrity you were arrested for menacing was Michael Portillo, whose eyesight is consistently portrayed on our screens as uncorrected, even when reading his Bradshaw. What's more, being cross-examined under oath, you were bound to confess your vitriol towards the thoroughly bespectacled Tim Wonnacott and utter ambivalence to Richard Osman.

But Chris, Mum? I could understand if it was Barry or Kevin.

~

Martin Strike's Biography

Raised from a pip by sophisticated goats, Martin is one of the lesser-known characters from Camberwick Green. These days he divides his time between blogging and imitating Tierra del Fuego, an archipelago off the tip of South America.

www.thenewburyshortstoryteller.wordpress.com

16: WHY IS GRANNY SO SMALL?

by Ciara Byrne

I ran to see my best, patterned friend and asked him, "Why is my granny so small? How come she is not tall like you, Goraff? How come she doesn't keep growing until she is high in the sky?"

Goraff answered, "Why, dear, my family keeps growing until we reach the tops of trees, until we can feel the rain drops before others, and until the ground and our feet are far away from our eyes."

I asked, "Will I not be tall when I am Granny's age? Granny seems to get smaller and smaller every time I see her, and I wonder why she doesn't grow taller and taller. She has been alive for such a long time and surely has been growing all this time. I have been growing tall – why not her?"

Goraff replied, "You will grow tall in spirit and character, higher than the sky and stars. You will fly with the birds, run with the cheetahs, swim with the elephants, but you or your granny will never grow tall like me or mine."

Disappointed, I ticked that question off my list. Now, I must go visit my best, stripy, friend – Zeeba.

~

Ciara Byrne's Biography

Ciara is a Dubliner who has been living in London for almost nine years. Although an ardent writer, from the snugness of her sofa, this is the first short story she has shared with the world.

17: HONEY DO

by D. Angelone

"Honey, I thought you were going to lift the curse today."

"I did."

"Then why's that thing still in our driveway? It's urinating again."

"What the–? Look, I punched the toad and squeezed my uncle's testicles, just like she said."

"Did you roll the corn in antifreeze?"

"Corn in the antifreeze, painted my toes with guano, I did it all."

"Did you make the macaroni Batman?"

"I did."

"And hang it on the fridge?"

"I'm not an idiot."

"Dave's?"

"Hmm?"

"Testicles. Dave's?"

"No, Frank's. Why?"

"She said your shortest uncle. God, I knew you would screw this up."

"Frank's my shortest uncle."

"Dave's like four feet tall."

"He's my uncle through marriage."

"Oh. Well, did you squeeze them under the pale moonlight?"

"Define 'pale'."

"Jesus, was it pale or not?"

"It was pale, ish."

"Wait. Did you drop the kids off?"

"Huh?"

"Please tell me you did that."

"Honey, she never said that."

"'When rooster crows twice, drop kids at noon, under freeway.' Verbatim."

"No, she said 'drop kick a nun'... under freeway."

"Do you have any idea how ridiculous that sounds?"

"Well, she had a strong accent."

"Don't talk to me."

"Honey..."

"I said don't."

~

D. Angelone's Biography

D. Angelone once stuck a peanut up his nose. Not one of the small bits that come in the can. A whole, fully shelled peanut.

18: UNREAD

by Peculiar Julia

William Ateeqi sits there, lonely as can be, wedged between Sara (5' 9" blonde and buxom) and Katia (fiery redheaded Amazonian, ready for anything).

He just doesn't understand. His language has been polite to the point of purple prose, his pleading sincere. He has everything to offer, but no one seems to care. No one in this place, anyhow. William feels ignored and, frankly, depressed.

What did you have to do to get attention around here? Has he been unclear about the urgency of the situation? Are his credentials not impeccable? He has news to make anybody's day – tidings of immense good fortune.

A sudden click and Katia spreads out, obscuring his view, then disappears as though folded into space. Where did she go? There must be an exit. She'd been lit up, then stretched, then gone.

Katia managed to get herself noticed, why not he? Is no one in need of 24 million US dollars?

Just a sec. The light again... It's hovering over... Sara... No, me – ME.

William is lit up with joy, wide open.

"My dear, I hope you won't betray my confidence in you. I am manager at the People's Bank of Nigeria..."

Move to Spam

~

Peculiar Julia's Biography

Julia is known for the rhyming of her name with peculiar. This is not the oddest thing about her. She loves to write, and wants to be read (sometimes – other times she just wants to hide under the blankets).

Find Julia on Twitter: @peculiarjulia

19: BURNT BEANS

by Cathi Radner

Tolliver Banks disappeared on a Tuesday. It didn't happen all at once. It seldom does. It began when he said, "Pass the butter," and no one noticed or offered a reply.

He liked it best when he was half-faded. Though the movies refused to give him half-priced tickets, when clearly he was only half there.

When Tolliver vanished completely, naturally, questions were asked. Heads were scratched.

"Ma'am," the police said to Tolliver's wife. "What has become of your husband?"

Shirley scratched her head. "I must have misplaced him. No bother. I never wanted one in the first place. It mustn't have been a good one, or I would have kept track. Though perhaps it was a good one, and I bought it half-off and never appreciated the value."

The police wrote this down, and then looked under beds and in closets. They found a small dog, which had nothing to say.

At dinner, Shirley said to her children, "Eat your peas," which they would have done, had there been any peas. They didn't like the buttered beans which were twice cooked over and burnt.

"Father never made us eat burnt beans," muttered the smallest.

Where is father? wondered the rest.

~

Cathi Radner's Biography

No author biography supplied.

20: THE POOR FIVE LOAFERS' WIDOWS

by Sandra Orellana

"Now who is going to put up with these loafers, or should I say widows?" said the first wife, sitting behind the other three widows. "Can you believe this vigil feast on New Year's Eve?" she continued. She loved the idea that 'The Show Goes On'.

She watched the young girlfriend widow on the front seat, sitting all alone. A young, dumb blonde, sobbing like a child in front of her fat boyfriend's casket.

The other three widows were just behind her. All three of them looked the same, with Botox treatments.

The three didn't say too much. In their mid-40's, with clone faces, they knew their lives would not be the same without talking about him, lost in their 'whacko minds', wondering what they were going to do or live for.

Suddenly, the young girlfriend-widow stood up and turned around and looked at the three ex-wives and said, "I'm lost without him. Could you advise me what to do?"

~

Sandra Orellana's Biography

Sandra Orellana is an American amateur writer who was born in El Paso Texas on the border of México.

Her passions are tennis, writing and reaching out to the most in need. She spends her time living in México City and San Miguel Allende.

21: A STABBING MYSTERY

by Olivier Breuleux

A woman laid face down in a pool of blood, a kitchen knife jutting out of her back. Inspectors Dim, Dum and Sum were on the scene hypothesising.

"The only other person with her at the time of her death was her dog," Dim said. "Therefore, the dog is the murderer."

"Astute," Dum agreed, stroking his smooth, shaven beard. "But the knife was found in the victim's hand. It must be a suicide."

"You are both wrong," said Sum. He proceeded to yank the knife out of the victim's back.

"Here is your murderer," he said, brandishing the blood-stained weapon. "Confess, swine," he intimated the knife, but it did not respond. "Confess, or I shall use you to cut jelly, pudding and aspic."

"NO. Anything but that. I admit it, I am the murderer," the knife confessed in its tinny, terrified voice. "But have mercy; Ms Rowd was the most terrible cook I had ever seen. Every day I was an accomplice to criminal soup. I had no choice but to kill her."

Sum walked to the pot in which a soup was simmering, and caught a whiff. It smelled like a legitimate defence.

~

Olivier Breuleux's Biography

Every night before dawn, Olivier roams sacred lands on

turtleback in search for faeries. He harvests their souls and shapes them into letters. This makes his stories truly magical and extraordinary, but you wouldn't know unless you read the originals.

www.outsideword.com

22: SORTED

by Annemarie Allan

The job of assistant biscuit organiser in the castle of King Nunn bored Mary Dilk to the point of tears. She was sobbing into the 27th tin when a packet of pink wafer biscuits exploded in a shower of sparkling crumbs.

"What's wrong with you?" asked Fairy Nuff, shaking the crumbs from her wand.

"I can't do this anymore," wailed Mary.

"Well, don't." The fairy reached for a chocolate digestive and munched vigorously. "The King never comes down here. He never sees the tins. Just chuck the biscuits in anyhow and make sure they're neat when you put them on the serving plate."

Mary laughed and wiped away the tears. "Fairy Nuff, you are an absolute genius." With the help of her friend, Susan Shocks, she finished her day's work in under half an hour. Fairy Nuff took care of the broken biscuits. Mary spent the afternoon with her boyfriend, Sam Handwich.

A few days after that, the King was delighted to discover that his people had begun to call him King Nunn the Wiser.

~

Annemarie Allan's Biography

Annemarie Allan was born in Edinburgh, lived briefly in California and then for much longer in London, before returning to Scotland, where she decided it was time to take her writing seriously.

Her first published novel, *Hox*, won the 2007 Kelpies Prize.

www.annemarieallan.com

23: 3 PHOBIAS

by Neville Raper

I have only three fears in my life, all rooted in childhood: ghosts, pirates and dentists.

In fact, if I ever bumped into the ghost of a pirate dentist, I'd probably kark it.

As a small boy I used to stay awake imagining spooks in my bed. My mum would hear my shivers and come into my room late at night to reassure me.

"There's no such thing as ghosts," she'd softly say.

I used to berate her, "Go away, Mum, you've been dead four years."

Dentists too, do you remember the school one? A distant descendant of Marquis de Sade.

When informed I had a cavity, he tried to cheer me up. "You can have a choice of filling," he offered. I asked for cheese and pickle.

Finally pirates, sailing the seven seas with one arm, one leg and one eye. They'd plague my dreams with their hooks and stumps. Flying a skull and crossbones, when it really should have been a disabled badge.

So there's the three. I've no doubt I'll develop more as life runs on. I leave you with one that I think I've just caught. Hippopotomonstrosesquippedaliophobia – the fear of long words.

~

Neville Raper's Biography

Broadcaster, author, occasional stand-up, regular sit-down.

Find me at The Thoughts of Chairman Anyhow on Blogger.

Find Neville on Twitter: @BenDeetoy

24: THE YODELLING PROFESSOR

by Jacob Derin

John was a professor at Ferguson University. He was a proud faculty member of old FU. He told people this fact with pride and joviality. He told his family, his friends, his acquaintances, and kept telling them long after they had asked him to stop. He had experimented with telling strangers in the street. As a result, he had been pepper sprayed not once, not twice, not five times, but thrice.

But, I digress. John's position of Professor of Yodeling was in serious jeopardy at his place of employment. It wasn't so much that he was disliked, the department head informed him. It was more the fact that there is no such job offered at the University. How, John countered, had he taught the subject for the past 15 years? His boss (of course, he would object to this title) simply shrugged his shoulders. He was very sorry, but there was no place for him at the university, it was policy.

John was upset, naturally, and slipped back into his old addiction: nose blowing. He indulged in it then, blowing a great deal of phlegm across the table. "Very well," John acquiesced, "I shall have to return to the coal mines."

~

Jacob Derin's Biography

No author biography supplied.

25: NOT SKATING ON THIN ICE

by Simon Humphreys

I'd always wanted to skate on the underside of a frozen lake. Having bought a pair of buoyancy skates to keep me upside down, I entered the world championships, being held the very next day.

Lake Takamo was the unlikely venue for this prestigious event. It didn't sound like a lake in Swindon, nor was it. As I jumped over the open gate, which led to the lake's edge, a man stopped me and bid me good day in Polish.

"Good day in Polish," he said.

I said nothing, but just scribbled the words 'don't tell anyone I'm here' on my forearm. I resisted the temptation to show him. *Ha*, I thought. *He'll never know I wrote all of that in lower case.*

It turned out that Lake Takamo was in Carlisle.

The competition was a disappointment. Being August, the ice was less than perfect – more like water really. Five competitors made up the entire world entry, although the other 16 had failed to enter. I did my best, but got eliminated by the only judge, who told me I could come back in three years and try again... in Polish.

"Come back in three years and try again, in Polish," he said.

~

Simon Humphreys' Biography

Simon Humphreys lives in Noordhoek, Cape Town. He

enjoys sailing his 1938 boat *Quest* in False Bay. His 'Cup of Tea' won first place in the Global Short Stories Competition in 2012. In 2016, Raging Aardvark Publications published his anthology of short stories entitled *Sandman*.

26: AND A VERY CHIRPY CHRISTMAS TO YOU TOO

by Sheila Corbishley

Mrs Santa marched with her shopping through the snowy park. Behind her, photographers in fur-trimmed parkas photographed rosy robins for next year's calendars.

"Beak open," they coaxed. "Fantastic. Now eye that mistletoe as if you really, r-e-eeally want it."

"It's disgusting," tweeted Mrs Robin, flying alongside Mrs Santa. "I mean – would you?"

"Perch on a spade? With my dodgy back?" snapped Mrs Santa. She was still peeved that, just before, she'd persuaded one of the photographers to take a saucy picture of her for Santa. He'd agreed so long as she was quick, but by the time she'd unwound her scarf, peeled off anorak, fleece and cable-knit jumper and was down to her thermal vest, she was sweating like a sautéd onion and the man was back to the robins.

"It's no joke being a woman of a certain age," she said bitterly.

"It's like you're invisible," sighed Mrs Robin. She nodded towards the shopping bags. "Got all your presents?"

"Just about. Except..." Blast. She'd got nothing for the cat. She looked sideways at Mrs Robin's plump little breast. "Fancy coming to mine for a nice Christmas drink?"

~

Sheila Corbishley's Biography

I'm Sheila Corbishley. I write short stories for adults, have won some competitions and had others published, and am feeling tentatively excited (many a slip etc.) because I've just had a children's story accepted by a small publisher.

27: THE DAY OF THE SPELL CHEQUE

by Helen Combe

Paul hated a threesome. Derek and Eve, the most ill-matched couple on the planet and him, down the pub. Derek put the tray of drinks down.

"Aw, Derek, you've got me the wrong drink," wailed Eve.

"It's a rum and coke."

"I asked for a Bacardi and coke."

"Same thing."

Paul zoned out and focused on the TV.

"We interrupt this programme to announce that the iPhone spellcheck and predictive text have achieved self-awareness and have escaped into the whirled."

Pall lucked at his eye phone. The screen was flashing 'Looser' at him.

"Hay, Guy Fawkes, eye mean guys, sum thing really wired, worried, woad, weird is happy hippy happening."

"Baccarat Backpack Bacardi is white, that's read."

"Gus, Guys the fabric of English is braking down!!!!!!!!!!!!!!!!!!!"

"Pall, stop doing awl those exclamation marks, their knot funny."

"!"

"Ewe never get yore drink wrong eye sea, Derrick," Eave foal died Durrell folded her alms.

"The fabric of thyme abs and space is braking down," Pall whaled.

Whither loud sucking nose nice noise, the whirled varnished vanished and Derrick and Eave whirr a loan in Nottingham, nothingness.

"Eye think the whirled has ended," said Derrick.

"It's all yore fault," said Eave.

~

Helen Combe's Biography

Helen is a member of Solihull Writers and was published in the prestigious *To Hull And Back Short Story Anthology 2016*. Her next proudest moment was being voted Ruler of the Universe at a sci-fi con as Servalan from *Blake's 7*.

www.facebook.com/SolihullWriters/

28: INCONGRUOUS EDIFICE

by Dean Walker

"Report. Light phase imminent. Predict hot dry."

"Report. Food levels adequate for standard growth."

"Our mind remembers previous light phase. Victory achieved in battle for Incongruous Edifice."

"Report. 50 percent loss to our battalion. Eight percent loss to total armada."

"Our mind orders an increase bias to military production."

"Our mind orders 40 percent of total armada to fight for Incongruous Edifice this light phase."

"Report. Termini suffered three to one loss."

"Our mind is happy with result. 40 percent will ensure complete victory over our enemy, the Termini."

"Our mind ponders the origin and structure of Incongruous Edifice."

"Report. Origin and structure remains unknown. Edifice has only one entrance and appears to be made of an extremely hard material. Alien in construction."

"Report. Edifice has one large cylindrical great hall. The floor holds very sweet food source."

"Our mind remembers. We have encountered many things we struggled to believe. We attacked and lost many to giant living constructs. We tasted nectar from the Avalon flower. All those memories can't compare to the food source Incongruous Edifice contains. We are humbled. We must have it."

The ant army marched in vast numbers. Three hours later, the cola can was theirs.

~

Dean Walker's Biography

My name is Dean Walker. I am a jeweller from Tasmania, Australia. I love reading and, while my hands are at play performing my trade, my mind is elsewhere making up stories. I've decided to start writing and share some of these ideas, as well as for my own sanity.

www.deanwalkerdesigns.com.au

29: THE ETHER

by Kathryn Meyer

"It's time for you to wake up now."

I smiled. I was awake. I realised I was cold.

"A blanket would be nice," I said.

I waited. No blanket arrived.

"You really need to wake up," a voice said.

"I am awake," I insisted. "And that one to ten thing you told me about beforehand? I'm approaching a nine. Maybe a shot of the good stuff to take the edge off?"

Again, I waited. No response. No blanket. No lessening of the increasing pain. Something had to be done.

"Wakey, wakey," a disembodied voice said.

Was I not making myself clear?

"I need pain medication," I yelled.

No response. I tried to open my eyes. They would not open. I tried to open my mouth. It seemed to be fused shut. Wait a minute. I must still be asleep.

"Doctor, I'm concerned," the voice said, anxiety colouring the words.

"Hold the pain medication," a deep voice said.

What? "No." I tried to protest, to no avail.

"Wake up," a voice boomed in my ear. A needle jabbed. A finger roughly forced my eyelid open and I saw my doctor peering down.

"Wake up," he repeated.

"But I am awake," I protested – to no avail.

~

Kathryn Meyer's Biography

No author biography supplied.

30: THE BATTLE OF THE BOWL

by Mark Fielden

Lemmy went out of the cat flap.
Goodness, gracious me, thought Nelly,
It's time for tea.
Where is my bowl?
Must I howl?
Before I get my tea?

Lemmy looked in through the cat flap,
Nell nowhere to be seen.
I hope her bowl,
From the bott'm of my soul,
Has food in it for me.

Lemmy hops in through the cat flap,
Leaps to Nelly's bowl.
But Nelly's there,
Behind the chair,
Produces a frantic howl.

Just one lick,
In just a tick,
Nelly's there behind him.
A couple of swipes,
At Lemmy's tripes,
The battle of the bowl.

The fur flies off,
A real standoff,
Lemmy looks for succour.
Nell smells blood,

You knew she would,
Warm flesh – it's time for supper.

But Lemmy spots a little gap,
Beneath the chair,
Where,
Nelly cannot touch herre. *[Lemmy is German; sad rhyming device – MF]*

The cat flap beckons,
So he reckons,
A launch into the air,
Will see him free,
From Nelly's tea,
His fur still on his knee.

A massive leap,
Down kitchen unit 600mm deep, *[Say it fast – MF]*
Escape comes his way.
The cat that leaps,
Doubtless saves a situation that would otherwise reduce his life count.

~

Mark Fielden's Biography

A young writer, halfway through my third 20-year career, so far my writing's been limited to technical manuals and operating instructions. Now I write web pages for a company that makes websites for authors with writing to sell. Oh, and I'm Chris's dad.

www.bluetree.co.uk

31: ODE TO THE HOUSE ACROSS THE STREET

by Anika Hussain

There is a garden full of white lilies where the father spends his final moments planting strawberries that will one day be pecked away by birds that give no concern for the care put into those figures of red.

There is a kitchen where the mother hums the tune to her favourite song, makes a meal for members who won't give her the time of day.

There is a bedroom, shielded with purple walls where the daughter cries her eyes out about a boy who cares too little, whilst pictures of who she used to be stare back at her in the sweltering September night.

At dinner they hold hands, say a prayer before delving into the nitty gritty details of the day, plaster on crescent moons where their lips used to be; pretend like they're not broken inside in their own ways.

Withstanding the flaming heat and the roaring snow, kids throwing eggs at Halloween, break ins and break outs: 11 by 11 meters; you hold a family intact.

~

Anika Hussain's Biography

I'm a 21 year-old writer based in Stockholm, Sweden. My writing focuses on the YA genre, gearing towards upper YA and realistic fiction. I have been published in smaller publications in both the UK and Sweden.

www.instagram.com/theuntitleddocument/

32: THE LEGEND OF SPICKETY SPOO

by Sim Smailes

Weep, weep away this gnarlish day, as painful news is spread. The end has come, the Odes are glum, for Spickety Spoo is dead.

He gave his all before his fall, the bravest of the brave. A hero he, a medal tree, no soul he could not save.

Against each foe he'd boldly go, no fear of guts or giblets. He brought back dead a Gorgon's head and sacks of scrawly niblets. Spoo slayed the Grix with lolly sticks, saved damsons in distress; his name hoorayed with lemonade in toasts of stickiness.

From dragon bats to giant rats each victory brought acclaim, until one day there came his way the Ice Hound of Chillblane.

Queen Maxipriest, chained by the beast, screamed out into the night. Then one, two, three Spoo set her free and charged with all his might. His cuttyslash snapped, Spoo now was trapped, but still he battled on. A final 'swish' then bony squish, the hero's life was gone.

Weep, weep away this gnarlish day, as painful news is spread. The end has come, the Odes are glum, for Spickety Spoo is dead.

~

Sim Smailes' Biography

Sim Smailes was born in Yorkshire, raised in Yorkshire

and loves Yorkshire. He now lives in Essex. He spends his time teaching and writing, trying to convince eight year olds that books are still worth reading.

33: THE POLITICIAN'S EXPLANATION

by Joseph Hancock

"I have been accused of certain unquestionable acts which may or may not have happened. These acts that I might not have perhaps quite possibly been involved with are without a doubt definitely of an uncharacteristic nature lying somewhere in the middle of true and not so true. It might be best to dissect these seemingly alarming acts and view them as an impossibility on my part seeing as I'm fairly uncertain these heinous creations might quite possibly have been designed in part by my opponents. These alleged allegations have vague connotations as to the potentiality of acts which could quite possibly have stemmed from doubtful and problematic natures that lay within the fabric of a lifestyle that is best described as easily unresolved.

"Now ladies and gentlemen we're all intelligent and thoughtful yet I'm if not unsure easily led to disbelieve that these unconscionable charges foisted upon me have been earmarked to harm my serious and exacting character no matter how capably ambivalent I am not.

"In closing allow me to render these forthright lies and seemingly uncertain truths to the rubbish bin with this simple impossibility as to my defense. I don't understand pillows. Thank you."

~

Joseph Hancock's Biography

Joe Hancock lives in Greenwich, Southern New Jersey, with his dog, Bug. A musician by trade, he is new to the writing field and loving every minute of it.

www.facebook.com/joseph.hancock.9480

34: A MATTER OF GREAT IMPORT

by Sarah Peloquin

Nothing of importance woke the prime minister. He opened his eyes on a grey, misty, Sunday morning, toddled out of bed, and completed his ablutions satisfactorily.

He meandered through the halls of Number 10 and joined his wife in the breakfast room. The coffee tasted off. He spat it back in his cup and ordered a new one from the kitchen. The second cup got the same treatment. He ignored the third one, miffed that his ordinary morning was disordered.

After services, he took his daily stroll in the garden, sniffed the roses, and noted a heaviness in the air. It would most likely rain that evening. His knees concurred, so he returned inside for a cup of tea and a warm fire.

The tea was as disappointing as his morning coffee. He pulled the cozy throw up to his neck and mumbled under his breath about incompetent help. His wife nodded her head absently as she knitted a Christmas stocking for their first grandchild.

She bade him goodnight around quarter to 11. He died at a quarter after, thinking it just his luck to not get a decent cuppa all day, and hoping for better on the other side.

~

Sarah Peloquin's Biography

Sarah Peloquin loves being the wife of her own knight in shining, but slightly dented, armour. Together they created three beautiful children – a princess, and two little princes. Sarah writes of life and love in the midst of her adventures.

www.srhplqn.wordpress.com

35: FARMS COLLIDE

by Melanie Rees

The pineapple exploded out of the machinegun, and splattered yellow pulp against a boab tree.

"Nice shot, Ace," snorted the camel. "You missed the target by a smoot."

"I was aiming for the tree." Ace dragged a claw though his red comb and adjusted his sunnies on his beak. "Still more productive than you. What is that anyway?"

"I'm weaving an asparagus basket to replace my leaking humps." The camel flung the basket onto her back.

Ace flew up and pecked at the basket. Asparagus spears fell, piercing the dirt.

"What did you do, you roving egg patsy?" The camel pulled an asparagus spear out of the dirt and milked mango juice from the wound like prized oil.

"Don't get your humps in a twizzle." Ace sipped the water leaking from her back. "It wouldn't hold water anyway."

An apple fell at Ace's feet.

"It's raining fruit salad again. Let's go back to the coup."

The camel grunted. "Fine, but I'm not walking back all that way."

"You lazy wannabe ruminant." Ace grabbed onto the camel and took flight. "Get your rest. I'm going to shoot an apple off your head with watermelons tomorrow."

~

Melanie Rees's Biography

Melanie Rees is an Australian author. Her fiction and poetry have happily and magically appeared in markets such as *Apex*, *The School Magazine*, *Aurealis* and Daily Science Fiction. Inquisitively, you can learn more on her website:

www.flexirees.wordpress.com

36: A RAT'S LIFE

by Solitaire

"Looks like I'm having dinner at your place tonight, Pam."

"No problem, Chester. I've plenty of everything now that my Lil' Bigfoot's passed on."

"Blast. I'm so insensitive. Pam, forgive me, I was busy with something or other that day."

"No biggie, Chester. We rats are always on the go."

"My fairy's fallen on hard times, Pam. And his lady fairy's upped and left him. Don't know when last he bought a good cheddar."

"They aren't fairies, Chester. They're humans. The cheese and crap they leave about aren't treats, as we've all believed. They're traps. They have no magic, they are evil. In fact many of them devote their lives to breeding CATS."

"Pam, you might be mourning, but the things you're saying are uncalled for."

"They're murderers, Chester."

"Pamela, you've been speaking to Larry, haven't you?"

"Larry makes a lot of sense."

"Pam, how can you trust a rat who first tasted cheese at the age of nine?"

"He used to be a prisoner in some lab where they did all sorts of tests on him. He's got more life experience than any of us common rats if you ask me."

"Pam, you're losing it."

~

Solitaire's Biography

Solitaire is a South African writer and award winning poet. He spends the majority of his days captivated by the wondrous occurrences in his imagination. Now and then he scribbles a few things down.

Find Solitaire on Twitter: @the1solitaire

37: WRONGSIDING THE DEMOGRAPHIC

by Mike Scott Thomson

It's All Hands On Deck for another Ideas Shower.

The Beverage Technician optimises the provision of Caffeinated Lifestyle Delivery Systems as we, the Internal Implementation Orchestrators, Touch Base Offline to Think Outside the Box.

The Senior Solutions Strategist rises from his seat to Fire the Starting Gun. "Going Forward," he says, "we must take the Helicopter View."

"The Grass has Grown Too Long," agrees the Principal Paradigm Planner. "How do we Square the Circle?"

"Put a Record On and See Who Dances," says the Future Functionality Engineer.

"Get All Our Ducks in a Row," suggests the International Integration Architect.

"Pick the Lowest-Hanging Fruit."

"Not Biting Off the Entire Elephant."

I suppress a coffee-flavoured burp.

The Senior Solutions Strategist points at me. "Something you'd like to Run up the Flagpole?"

"Yeah," I snap. "You."

He looks puzzled. "Could you Drill that Down?"

"Yeah," I repeat. "I wish to wedgie your Y-fronts up to your armpits and run YOU up the flagpole, you overwrought, overpaid, pompous, purple-faced gasbag of gobbledegook."

A pause.

"You're sacked," he blurts.

"That," I say, as I make my welcome exit, "is the most sensible thing I've heard all day."

~

Mike Scott Thomson's Biography

Mike Scott Thomson's short stories have been published by journals, anthologies and have won the occasional award, including first prize in Chris Fielden's inaugural To Hull & Back competition.

Based in south London, he works in broadcasting.

www.mikescottthomson.com

38: BUBBLY-WUBBLY ROW

by Ian Richardson

"I don't think we can call our inter-web homepage Anti-Technology Websites," whispered Ned Ludd, after the bubbly trailers.

"Why not?" hissed Auntie Pro. "It says what we are... captures our whole bubbly-wubbly ethos."

"In short," announced Lady Portman Hoverboard Ann Lodging the Second, "that name his too long."

"How about ATW?" blubbered Auntie Pro, staring at the wall, as they watched all the whales, all the while.

"Just another TLA," muttered Ned Ludd, picking at his bubble stitched boatneck sweater until it frayed, "I'm afraid."

"In short," repeated Lady Portman Overboard the Second, for the second time, "hi think this is taking far too long. Hi think we need to finish before this starts."

"TLA's a TLA," protested Auntie Pro, as the Fresnel bubbles dimmed again.

"Ssssh," hissed Lady Portman II. "Sorry to burst your bubble – there will be no Three Letter Abbreviations. Hi need something punny."

"New Luddites," cried Ned Ludd, spluttering bubbly into his supersized movie cup. "Nu-luds."

"Antipro," exclaimed Auntie Pro, rather too loudly.

"Auntie Pro... Antipro... a portmanteau," repeated Lady Portman Two. "Get me my bag of popcorn and go."

~

Ian Richardson's Biography

Ian Richardson lives on the East coast of Scotland.

In 2016 his works were published in *RAUM poetry*, *Eildon Tree* and *Temporal Discombobulations*.

He is a regular contributor to the 'Lies and Dreaming' spoken word podcast.

www.jukepop.com/home/read/105

39: WITHOUT MY BIG TOE

by Barry Smith

My body needs help to do things. This is down to me having a physical disability which is cerebral. People look at me so differently. I am a person who likes to try.

Teaching myself new skills feels so good. My hands jump around. Using things to make up for this feels so good too. Toes can type on the computer. It feels so nice and I feel so helpful too.

My body can wake up. I don't like to do it, but sometimes I need to, because sometimes people don't see me for who I am.

~

Barry Smith's Biography

I have Cerebral Palsy, which is a physical disability. I use a power wheelchair to get around when I am out, but when I am in my house I move around on my bum. Many people can't do this.

40: THE MAMBLE JOTTERS

by Vanaja Shankar

Lam Jotter was so tall that when he stood near the mamble tree he could see the bird's nest. The spotty bird feeding juicy mambles to the young ones glared at him. "Squeak. Squeak. Why do you peep?"

"I am plucking a purple mamble fruit for Mrs Jil Jotter," he burbured.

"A mamble fruit gives you what you mumble," giggled the bird.

Jil Jotter deeled in squilight. She loved eating because she had nothing else to do.

Jil Jotter was so fat, she couldn't see her toes.

Lam had grown tall stretching to pluck fruits.

"I saw the spotty bird feeding the little ones," Lam laughed.

"I wish we had two bubbly kids," Jil mumbled.

There was a swish and a swash, a peel and a squeal.

Two mamble fruits turned into children, bobbing up and down.

"Welcome home Parry Jotter and Norry Jotter," squealed Jil in joy.

Parry and Norry bounced on the table like two balls. Jil ran around trying to catch them.

"I wish they'd grow taller and fatter," mumbled Jil.

Parry grew one inch taller and Norry one inch fatter every day.

Jil became thinner and Lam became shorter and they all lived happily ever after.

~

Vanaja Shankar's Biography

Vanaja Shankar is a banker, corporate trainer, and writer. Her book *Hello Banker* is a collection of short stories about the lives of young bankers. She is passionate about reading and writing women's fiction.

She also enjoys writing nonsense.

www.vanajashankar.com

41: THE SUPERIOR INSIGHT OF THE SOZZLED MS C

by Ian Tucker

Buzzing bells boomed in the bonce of boozy bloodhound Delia Celia as she interrogated the laughing corpse of the poisoned cellist. The gumshoe knew there'd be no clue who'd slew Lou McGrew in the new zoo's loo. But something about the rictus grin and split sides of those great barrier teeth was dead funny.

Seedy P.I. DC mused on the malevolent motives of the minstrel's menagerie. What of the bitter morbidity of the Bleak Mouse or the envious greed of the Yellowbrick Toad? Could the Damp Squid or the Red-Bottomed Baboom be at the heart of the attack?

And how was it done? The flying Ostrich, sitting astride the standard, stroked the golden goose and glowered at the pacing of the lying Westrich. The lady dick speculatively stroked her stubble.

The Sudden-Tern-for-the-Worse dived impetuously.

"You, Tern," the sleuth slurred, "what did you see?"

The Nasty Tern squawked like a canary, denying everything. Dissolute D discerned a lightbulb, darkly, and raised a glass. Clearly, the musical mark was murdered seeking, unseen, to shed light in a dark place. Death by deadly lampshade.

Dizzy dazed Delia directly denounced the devious Ostrich whose failed flight left it doing bird at Sing Sing.

~

Ian Tucker's Biography

Ian is a writer when he has a chance and an idea as well as a desire to entertain himself. He is well practiced in nonsense. There are stories by him at:

www.tilebury.com

42: THE SECRET LIFE OF WALTER RALEIGH

by Trevor Johnson

Walter Raleigh walks into a pub. At the bar there's Christopher Columbus, Francis Drake and Long John Silver.

"Hi, Franc. Long time no see."

"Walt, how've you been?"

"Not bad. What've you been up to?"

"Oh, the usual, sailing around the world."

"Seen Liz recently?"

"Yes. When was Liz in here, Long John?"

"Liz? Who be that then?"

"You remember Liz, had that dress with the high collar, ordered half a lager and a bag of pork scratchings."

"Ah, Liz, Queen of the virgins. Last Tuesday I'm thinking it be."

"She asked if I'd seen you."

"What did you tell her?"

"Don't worry, I kept your secret about America."

"Oh, a secret, eh?" says Columbus.

Walter blushes. "Nothing."

"If you've got something going in America, you've got me to thank for discovering it."

"I met this woman in New Orleans."

Columbus persists. "What's her name?"

"It's... Joan."

"Joan... Joan... New Orleans... not Joan from the Arc seafood restaurant?"

"Yes, Joan of Arc. Do you know her?"

"Many have *known* Joan," smirked Columbus.

"Cheer up Walt," says Drake. "It's not the end of the

world."

"I thought it was when I arrived in America," says Columbus.

~

Trevor Johnson's Biography

Trevor Johnson has directed and acted in plays ranging from Oscar Wilde to Alan Ayckbourn. His publications include a play *My Ex*, a novel *Sorry's Not Enough* (Amazon), and two collections of short stories *Trevor's Shorts* (Amazon).

www.trevorjohnson.net

43: THE WONDER OF DOCTOR CLAUDACIOUS FUDD'S ASTOUNDING AUTOMATON

by Trudy Utterly

With one last twist of the screwdriver, it was done.

"Aha," Dr Fudd exclaimed, "they all thought I was mad, said it couldn't be done, but after 30 years of tinkering – here it stands."

His beady eyes narrowed above his bespectacled nose to inspect his schematics one last time.

One vulcanised positronic microtronic zap adapter... check.

One revolving megakegazegachip... check.

A set of super electro-neutronical bulbs... check.

And finally, one blinker optic broadbending rubber-tipped multiprocessor... check.

It was ready – the world's first artificially intelligent robot with the capacity to think of thinkables, equipped with an intellect to far exceed anything any mere mortal has ever contemplated in the history of contemplation.

The Doctor's fidgety fingers now tantalisingly tingled whilst they dipped into the skull lid to switch on the machine.

The automaton began to clink and chuggle. Inside, spinny things began to spin, cogs began cogging and zaps began zapping.

Its electronic eyes lit up, now it began to fathom the unfathomable.

"It's alive."

The doctor watched in awe and terror as the automaton's robotic arm began to rise, its mechanical fingers reached into its skull lid... and promptly turned itself off.

~

Trudy Utterly's Biography

Science-fiction nerd, avid reader, micro-fictionist and author of *The Little Book of Cosmic Nursery Rhymes*, Trudy Utterly is an independent writer from the West Midlands. An enthusiast for English language and quirks.
Find Trudy on Twitter: @TrudyUtterly

44: A FABLE

by S.T. Ranscht

Our nog hatched from a little egg, its feathers soft and brown. But every time we washed it clean, it shed more eiderdown. Its balding patches soon revealed its skin was scaly gold.

"Oh, woe," the neighbors all bemoaned. "Just kill it," we were told.

"But why?" we cried, "we love our nog."

"But it's not smooth and pink. It won't be long before its pores give off a righteous stink. The deadly azure parasites will come to suck its blood. They love the smell that emanates from all that golden crud. Pink-skinned nogs sometimes attract the blacks, which are benign, but never has a gold survived the blue malignant kind."

We searched the world to find a cure against the sucking bugs. Like acupuncture, herbal teas, and new Big Pharma drugs.

A wizened elder in Nepal knew one last thing to try. "It's possible a leech on each might cause the bugs to die."

But bleeding failed, and little Nog fell victim to the pricks.

It broke our hearts to learn the truth:

You can't leech a gold nog's blue ticks.

~

S.T. Ranscht's Biography

Ms Ranscht lives in San Diego, California, avoiding winter and Stephen King's pompously ridiculous writing advice. She's had three short stories published in anthologies for charity. Hopefully, her YASciFi novel, *Enhanced*, will soon find an agent, publisher, and financial success.

www.stranscht.com

45: IN CONCLUSION, IT SEEMS ONLY LITTLE GIRLS CAN CLIMB STARS

by Emma-Karin Rehnman

We reached the end in just four months. As the excellent explorer and scientist I am, I naturally noted and wrote down behavioural changes in my odd little travel partner. For the last week, she had been acting a little strange.

"We've got to tie our shoes better," she told me several times a day. "And eat lighter food. Bread with air bubbles in it, and meringues, and, and..."

"Cheese?" I suggested, but gently – she seemed a bit upset. Cheese is a food with holes in it, but apparently it was not light enough for her games, for she screamed at me.

Then we got to the end. The sky met the ground, and I hit my head on it before she did, as I am taller. It was surprisingly hard, the star clad dome.

"Oh boy." And I thought she never got nervous. "Hope my food's been light enough."

She put her little foot on one star, and her hand on one slightly above her head – and she climbed. With every movement she went further into the sky, and no matter how I tried, I couldn't follow.

"Bye, mister," she yelled. "Growing up was a really bad idea."

~

Emma-Karin Rehnman's Biography

No author biography supplied.

46: TEST PAPER

by Coryn Smethurst

For this paper you must have:
1. a pencil
2. mathematical instruments
3. a large cucumber

An insert containing NO useful information is provided.

Time allowed: 24 hours.

Instructions:

- Use a white pen or invisible ink – do not use anything which is legible
- Fill in the boxes at the top of this page with pictures of Philip Schofield
- Answer questions on one topic only:
  - Topic A: Reticulated Pythons, Puff Adders and Theresa May
  - Topic B: Warts, Verrucas and Phil Hammond (with reference to almonds)
  - Topic C: Nick Gibb, Statistics and Money Laundering (with biological detergent)
  - Topic D: History of Buxton, Nicky Morgan and Musical Flatulence
- Answer all questions on the topic you have chosen, but be careful the chocolate does not melt
- Write your answers anywhere you wish, but remember the cheese does not melt on Saturday
- Do not think outside the box around each page, but do think on blank pages

- You will be marked on your ability to:
  - subvert the English language
  - disorganize information in a clear manner
  - use specialist vocabulary relating to trousers, where appropriate

Remember that anything you write will be regarded as wrong.

~

Coryn Smethurst's Biography

Coryn Smethurst is a philosopher working with words, sound, and vision.

He is a multiple award winning wildlife sound recordist, and the chief organiser / co-founder of the Sonic Arts Forum:

www.facebook.com/groups/sonicarts/

47: THE EYES HAVE IT

by Allen Ashley

Mother's way of calming me down was to whisper, "Look into my eyes and say 'pickle'." Later I learned that the eyes are the window to the soul and that the night has a thousand eyes. Somehow I doubted that the night also possessed a thousand souls. But it was dark so I couldn't be sure.

On the lash with some mates, my eyes were always bigger than my belly. I must have presented a frightening sight, all googly and staring like two pickled onions. No wonder the supermodel-thin women never came my way.

I was the apple of mater's eye; grown to become mostly a consumer of eye candy. I kept my eyes peeled, disposing of the skin shavings in a temporary fashion by stuffing them up my pullover sleeves.

In raucous mood at the local hostelry, one my pals quipped, "Here's mud in your eye." Panicking, I pulled my pullover and dabbed with my skinny sleeve. The effect of me pulling the wool over my own eyes was that there wasn't a dry eye in the house. I tried to close my eyes and think of England but I was hungry. I ordered a Ploughman's – bread, cheese and pickle.

~

Allen Ashley's Biography

Allen Ashley is the author or editor of 14 published books. Most recent is an updated, revised version of his novel *The Planet Suite* (Eibonvale Press, 2016). He works as a creative writing tutor and critical reader.

www.allenashley.com

48: WHAT DO YOU DO WITH A DRUNKEN QUAVER?

by Estella Andres

"Places please," boomed the horn, each sound swathed in disapproval.

The pieces of music continued to writhe and weave across the page, setting the violins off, screeching as they tried to interpret the ever-changing pattern.

At last finding their places, the quavers wavered so fiercely, creating so violent a tremolo across the staff that it caused the crotchets to be dislodged from their perches like plump pigeons off telephone wires.

Again, the crotchets would clamber up threatening to unseat the wobbling apologetic quavers, clinging one-armed to their line, jostling the semi-breve open-mouthed at the appalling behaviour and the breve flung its arms up in disgust.

"I am trying," each giggled.

"Well, at least they're still pitch perfect," trilled the clarinet.

To which the timpani did a drum roll.

~

Estella Andres' Biography

No author biography supplied.

49: SNIZZLING TINO

by Zaheer Babar

"Aboo," snizzled Tino the Manratop.

"Hibble-Who," replied the Anran, who was sitting at a desk nearby. "Are you catching the strot?"

"No, I'm just snizzling, I'm always snizzling when I come to work," professed Tino.

"Aaboo," Tino snizzled the second time.

"You must be plurgic to something."

Tino took out a small ramaal and blew his pinkle with it. A few seconds later his pinkle started to tinkle. He tried to hold it in but to no avail. "Aaabooo," he cried, honzler and flizzler than before. He could not help but spray progbas everywhere, all over his desk and notepad.

"Hibble-Who, look who's got the strot," chimed in a passing foggle.

"That's what I thought," agreed the Anran.

Tino was embarrassed by the attention his snizzling was getting him and endeavoured to find the cause of his slight. He noticed a flower by the corner of his desk in full bloom. *That must be it, I must be plurgic to it*, thought Tino. He then persisted to remove the flower from his vicinity. He sniffed the air with apprehension. Nothing, not even a tinkle and Tino breathed in a sigh of relief.

"Aboo," went the Anran.

"Hibble-Who," chuckled the Manratop.

~

Zaheer Babar's Biography

Zaheer Babar the Manratop was born in Pakistan and moved to the UK when he was less than two years old. Bred and living in Worcester, England, he is married with four children. He is still snizzling to this day.

50: CAPTAIN BEANY VERSUS THE DARK GARLICK

by Captain Beany

Our half-baked crusading superhero, Captain Beany from Planet Beanus, surveyed the 57 heavenly varieties on a bitterly cold and chilly bean night. All of a sudden, a strange globular apparition slowly emerged from the sauce and lit sky above.

"Oh no," cried out the Captain. "Not another invasion by that dreadful dissident... that Dark Garlick from Planet Garlicka."

"I am a Garlick, I am a Garlick," bellowed the sinister destroyer. "I am here to breathe new life onto your trumped-up planet, and you, Captain Beany, are going to become one big has-bean."

"Not if I can help it. I'm gonna blow the wind out of your sails," revelled the Captain. "Now... watch this you big bulbous baboon."

Prostrating his superhero orange pants at the ghastly grotesque featureless clove, the Captain mustered one of the biggest methane gaseous farts that he could ever conjure up, but in fervent retaliation, the halitosis half-breed brandished his very own toxic pungencies from his horrid 'orrible orifice.

Whiff War One commenced at full-blown fart-ocity and, after much heavy flatulent emission slaying, the desperate Dark Garlick finally exploded into garlic powder and dissipated into the misty fuggish air.

"That shall teach you not to play with fire," said the jubilant Captain. "That Dark Garlick is now well and truly pulverised."

~

Captain Beany's Biography

Captain Beany from Planet Beanus is a half-baked crusading superhero who is currently on a 'full blown' mission to 'baldly go where no man has BEAN before' for the 'beanefit' of mankind – and may the force go behind you all.

www.captainbeany.com

51: A HARD DAY'S NIGHT

by David Ormerod

The sun sank below the waves sending up a plume of steam which, in the blink of an eye, slowly formed into a brooding cloud.

"Oh great, rain," complained Colin the mermaid, stomping across the raft's parade ground and disappearing downstairs.

The stairs led up to a tunnel which snaked its way pointlessly into the bright sunshine of Colin's bedroom.

Collecting his mop from the floordrobe, he squished a block of squid ink onto its bristles, put it away again and began.

"Soon have you back out there blinding the moles," he told the sun, gently scrubbing behind it's ears with considerable force.

He worked all night then got out of bed, wandered to his bedroom and hauled on the chains, dragging the sun out into the dismal light of a bright new day.

"Oh, not this again." The sun squinted up at the Earth, it's people still busy in bed ignoring him. Their brilliance shone upwards, reflected from his brightly mirrored features, causing a happily threatening shadow to spread across the choppy waves of the calm sea, swamping Colin's raft, then darting sluggishly down into the pea-blue gloom, taking all their secrets with them.

~

David Ormerod's Biography

David Ormerod is a keen writer, currently working on his novel *Hard Reign*, an exciting, fast-paced historically accurate novel set on the Anglo Scottish border during the tumultuous year of 1296. You can contact him via Facebook:

www.facebook.com/profile.php?id=100014968779473

52: FLIBBERTS AND SKRIDDICKS

by Sarah Aston

Amongst the flibberts and skriddicks that my parder left me when he ebbed was his squaliday home. My marter had never visited it, nor had I. It was half-way up the chill to the hurch in Tidy on the Dye.

After the kithkeening, I had to visit to sort out his benequeaths. I expected to be lousterin' his vanitairs and renderings enderendedly, but things were surprisingly beladdered.

The scruntings had been watered, the polkers were clean and cornered and the retinographs were all in order of yearnings.

In the middle of the panteroom was a low squable that I remembered giving my parder on his third rememebering. On it was a trimbling pinnyraid maundering gently.

"Oh purty chy, what's mine is thy."

I hesitated but the maundering became more clamicant so, stirring all my puissance, I asked the pinnyraid to unpanter itself.

It did and inside was just one small bulbling. My parder had loved his alittlement and kintindid that he could make anything blooth. The thought made me muty arted and my selspots fell onto the bulbling. It trimpered, then snickered and then a newmicorm was before me. The fourth remembering. My parder was returned to me.

~

Sarah Aston's Biography

Sarah lives in rural Wiltshire. After a long career in management she wants to get back to using her imagination. Sarah's always written songs but this is her first attempt at a story. For that she thanks/blames Mark.

53: A MEAL FIT FOR THE PEOPLE

by Stephanie Sybliss

The House of White stood sturdily, waiting for the warmth that was OB to leave. The windows closed and darkness descended, tumbling down the staircase. It spread throughout the building and the area that was once full of candour with the veracity of truth, rapidly became riddled with an air of sticky jus.

It coated everything in its wake. The dark, gravy-like substance was hard to shift. Never again would the honourable, decent, filled cupcake of truth be something people would ever taste again.

The building that had stood for something the diners had grown to love and believe was, in the blink of an eye, becoming tainted with the coat of DT.

They had once opened the oven door to a sumptuous meal that everyone could enjoy and now they were going to have to dine on the bones of rotting food and the detritus that was beginning to sprout from the towers of DT, slowly seeping into the House of White.

OB is moving out and DT is swiftly moving in his Men of Yes, who are full of flamboyancy and sludge.

They plan to cook up some meals full of distortion and fabrication for us all.

~

Stephanie Sybliss's Biography

It's wonderful to talk nonsense at times and even better

to write nonsense that someone wants to publish. I guess I'm just living the dream. Thanks for the opportunity.

My Blog, Thoughts from a Black Girl's Diary, can be found here:

www.wordpress76354.wordpress.com

54: FOUR WAYS TO SAY I LOVE YOU

by Ken Goldman

He did not go down on one knee. That was for amateurs. "I want to marry you. I love you."

She smiled. "Do you? Prove it."

He pulled a small pocket knife from his jeans and cut off his pinky finger. He handed the digit to her. "How's this?"

"Impressive. But only the pinky? You won't miss it."

He swathed the remaining stub in a cloth. Cutting off his index finger, he handed that to her as well. "And now?"

She studied the two bleeding digits. "Better. But you still have two remaining piggies that haven't gone to market, plus a thumb."

He shrugged, and this time he did grimace. He cut off his thumb and ring finger, wrapping his hand in the soaking cloth. "I prefer to keep the middle piggy home, if you don't mind. So, will you marry me now?"

The woman laughed long and hard. "Marry you? What makes you think I would marry a man who is into self-mutilation? You must be a complete idiot." She laughed some more.

"I was afraid of this," he said. "Well then..."

He held up the remaining middle finger, waved it before her face, and walked off.

~

Ken Goldman's Biography

Ken Goldman is a former Philadelphia high school teacher of English and Film Studies, with stories in over 850 independent press publications and five books to his credit. He lives in Penn Valley Pennsylvania and at the South Jersey shore.

55: FINDING THE MEAN

by June Lee

Straightening his tie and twisting his neck as if it were sore when it really wasn't were two of his well-practised pre-game rituals. It was time.

Announcing yet another crackdown on major crime, the Lakes District Mayor stared earnestly down the camera lens with a gaze of undisguised loathing and in his best 'we've been in City Hall for two terms and have no plans to leave anytime soon' voice intoned, "I have a message for the so called criminal mastermind known as Evil Maths Genius or EMG for short – your days are numbered."

~

June Lee's Biography

June Lee's work has appeared in *Pure Sludge*, *The Don't Bother Review*, *Dross Monthly*, *Garbage Hole*, *Dreadful Fiction*, *Regrettable Reads*, *Take Pity Magazine*, *The Poor Press*, *D Class Scribes*, *Leftover Quarterly* and *Useless Words*.

She is forthcoming in *Give It A Miss*.

June Lee is known for her consistent use of the unreliable narrator.

56: PRAPS CHRISTMAS WON'T COME

by William Chris Sargeant

Decembermonthster panted heavily through winding Novemberalleystrats. He was surely arriving late. No one else could take up or wanted his burdensome slothtime.

He carried his allotted 31daybits but always had the heavier religionaddays of Christmas and other festives on his back.

These destinweights of Christmas, caused tinsels and lights to glint his steaming body reds, blues, silvers.

So unfair, he thought, *other monthsters shared the extra burdens of the moonsundriven Easter and fetevots*.

He'd served a long hard slothtime last year. Spartying had taken toll. He dallied through into Janssloth, then stayed on at Febsbrewery, drinking until given his Marchingon orders.

He'd showered with cold April hoping he Mayed it to the sistermonthsters Juni and Julie, but summer heat began to rot his baggage and nauseate his surrounds so, with no resting, he hurried forward to his slothtime.

Disoriented, he got lost in Septembermonthsters leafful, blustful avenues.

Signpostings hidden, he'd stumbled sideways into black holes of memory and was heading for the before year's slothtime until, with the help of TimeDad, he was reguided forward.

Snowfully breathless he was now almost there. Urged by a slitted moonshine, his slothtime was dawning fast. He might not make it this year. Praps for the best.

~

William Chris Sargeant's Biography

For my grand and great-grand skirthle and panthle monthsters April, Jan, June, Chris and especially for just arrived Julie.

57: MR SANDERS AND THE PARKING LOT DRAGON

by Charlie Hills

Mr Sanders stepped out of the car, his left foot plunging into a puddle. "Not again." He shook the water from his shoe and began walking when he heard a rumbling sound. Was that thunder? No. It sounded more like... it couldn't be. An animal growling that loudly would be ginormous.

He continued when the sound became unmistakable. He turned to see a dragon with a nasty look in its eye. Mr Sanders froze, not quite as worried about his drenched sock. The dragon moved closer. Mr Sanders' mind raced. *I could run*, he thought. *Or call for help*. The dragon roared. "Think, think," he said, before realising he must fight.

He opened his briefcase and pulled out a sword and armour. *And I almost didn't pack this stuff this morning*. The dragon was upon him. Mr Sanders raised his weapon, but the beast was too quick. In one swipe, his sword was gone. A formidable claw raised itself for a fatal blow, when Mr Sanders picked up his briefcase and quickly slammed it shut around the dragon.

Sadly, the thrill of victory was curtailed when a horrible thought entered his mind. *I bet he eats my lunch.*

~

Charlie Hills' Biography

Charlie Hills is the author of zero novels. He's trying to fix that. In the meantime, check out some of his non-fiction work:

www.charliehills.com

58: HAPPINESS IS A WARM ERTEDLE

by Amy Stanton

Just out of curiosity, Miriam logged in to her twin sister's idatings.com account. 42 unread messages. How did she have so many? They created their accounts at the same time. Miriam only had 15 messages, all mere spam or catfishing. No cultive love matches. She tried to squelch her feelings of ruptissitions, but they summenced regardless. Miriam and Mairim were identical. Tall blonde beauties with wagibbley figures.

Miriam scrolled through the messages and randomly opened one from LaPlayaGent. Before she could even read the message, she was 'treated' to his provile photo: a shaved and oiled up muscle-bound torso, no head in sight.

Miriam stifled her resphetting reflex, and read on:

Hey beautiful, how about you and I share a bottle of cadazz and sching it on. Love to see what colour of cobints you have on under that bodiss you're wearing – if any, hehe.

Text me.

Miriam nearly lost the battle with her resphetting reflex. The urge was strong. If all the messages were like this, Mairim could have them. Miriam opened a new browser window and looked for an ertedle to adopt.

~

Amy Stanton's Biography

No author biography supplied.

59: RELINQUISHED REGARD

by James Butt

Mr Coffee you burn me, brewer of mourning, my Monday mug third in the line of three. I'm third but present.

"Hey." Earnest Callow, second, spoon in hand, enters behind me.

I freeze, unwilling to fall victim to the redundancies required by this civility. Don't say it. And Mr Coffee gurgles, chokes. Don't say it, please.

"How 'bout this weather, huh? Great weekend too, you do anything?" Earnest asks, filling his mug direct from the drip.

I search my pockets for a phone to escape this peculiar subtlety. I find no phone. My only reproach is to utter, "Yes, how 'bout this weather?"

"I know, cold, but the perfect cold, you know? Later."

I strike tones of discordant rhythm with my spoon, the beat, beat. Mr Coffee you burn me, a deuce of fact and I wait the line.

~

James Butt's Biography

James Butt lives in Nova Scotia, is forgetful of the past, confused by the present, worried about the future, and writes to make sense of it all.

60: CULINARY CHAOS

by Wendy Christopher

The impeccable courgette was celebrating his life choices, but Victoria Sandwich wanted more from life than a flaunting of jam and cream. His was a vegetable tyranny, stealing the thunder and making the lightning cry when it sang The Carpenters' greatest hits. Oh, such misery. She watched him sashay among the cucumbers with vinegar and balsamic in her heart. His moustache was cute, but he could never carry off the pinstriped trousers like them.

How had they ended up together in this eternal tea-time?

Too often she would look back, but all she saw was salt and pepper. They kissed because they were ignorant, and she knew if she became the trois in their ménage they would ruin her. Only a courgette so cruel as to hide in salad could savour her sweet nature. So here she doilied, a slave to a life of cheap frills with a fruit incognito who sponged off her. He was not what people thought he was, but then neither was she. She was split down the middle, but that didn't mean she belonged in a lunchbox.

"I will let Courgette have me," Victoria whispered softly, "but he will not devour me as well."

~

Wendy Christopher's Biography

No author biography supplied.

61: THE DEVIL'S GUITAR

by Jason Dunn

"If I can play even a simple chord, I am set free," he announced to the crowd.

His velvet red suit jacket fitted him divinely: deep pockets, fireproof and stuffed with the severed heads of mice.

"I built this guitar to be accursed. Absolutely no one can play it. But can I?"

His perfectly manicured hand reached into the right front pocket and extracted from an open mouse head a single black, obsidian guitar pick. It shimmered in his dusty grip and reflected the bright orange-red campfires nearby in streaks and sparkles.

A bead of sweat rolled down his forehead. He looked across the crowd. A sea of sockets and mouths gaped back at him, their hollow expressions all that remained of their humanity. Yet despite their endless misery, they found a glimmer of curiosity this day, and managed to gather to hear the devil play.

"It's a crow's song, I'll wager," shouted some British woman in the back.

"What would the devil name a song even he cannot play?" asked a withered, pitiful murderer of a woman, with silvery black hair, bows and going on her 400th year of hypopituitarism.

All strings broke and the guitar laughed.

~

Jason Dunn's Biography

No author biography supplied.

62: IN SEARCH OF A JOKE

by S.W. Hardy

"Argh, rats," said the Cat to the Bat, who try as he might couldn't take flight because he was anti-light. "Can't you see that between you and me there is Bee?"

"Be that as it may, that there may be – maybe – a Bee, between you and me," said Bat, before abruptly jumping in fright, and gliding like a kite, because even in the dead of night he could see that a Bee which had faint aromas of tree wafting from its knee had materialised out of nowhere, or was it thin air? Did he really care?

"It's me," said the Bee, "and I can see the key, upon which we float like a boat, in the middle of the sea of fleas, just west of the rest of the crests, which inhabits the nest of the best jests."

"So, you're in search of a joke," spoke the aquatic-flea-folk, "we have one bespoke, guaranteed to make you choke with happy tears for years and years, so we shall raise our flea-beers and say 'flea-cheers' to the humour, which is only a rumour until we tell you the punchline in the future."

~

S.W. Hardy's Biography

I graduated from the University of Nottingham with a degree in Creative Writing. I self-published my first Young Adult novel *No Separation* (available on Amazon) and run a travel/writing website. I currently live and

teach in Shenzhen (China).
www.swhardywriter.com

63: DEATH AT THE DOOR

by James Hendy

A whirr and a tinkly-tonk and the jilluping red jelly doorbell had been hammered by the sledgamoose, the only one left of its furry, 3.5 armed, kind. It was a dangerous creature with eyes that breathed fire and a mouth that constantly glared. It was ruthless and nobody liked it.

On the other side of the door, sat in a five-legged cloud-clad armchair, was the delicate bobbit. She had long pasta locks and laughed like a tickled lizard. She was kind and innocent and in love with life.

Having heard the cacophony of the seldgamoose, the whirlscratching bobbit harrumphed herself to the big blue bashful door.

She peaked through the peaky-poky nispytrisk and saw the huge brick monster, looming over her tender popcorn house. The house whinnied and scuttled frantically nowhere.

The beast hammered again and made the doorbell wobble like the ears of a didlywhop fish.

The door creeped open.

Poor bobbit thought she was going to die and quivered.

The door creaked some more.

The beast began to grin.

The door swung open and with a triumphant, "Hubbaldibblydoo," the bobbit shot the mean sledgamoose in its horrible face. It died. All was good again.

~

James Hendy's Biography

No author biography supplied.

64: PRIDE COMES BEFORE A FALL

by Klaus Gehling

The policemen was standing on his platform in the avenue and was regulating the traffic. He seemed to be very unapproachable.

But something ripped into his heart every day. This wonderful, great avenue was empty. No vehicles, even bicycles, passed by.

For crying out loud. An ox-drawn cart was creeping onto his crossing – an ox team on the avenue. They stopped in front of him.

After a seemingly endless time one of the oxen began to poo. Before the policeman fell forward from shock, he thought, *What a nasty smell*.

"I know how fast these things can happen," comforted his mother later.

~

Klaus Gehling's Biography

Klaus is a retired psychologist and psychotherapist living in Germany. He spends his time writing stories, playing chess and his guitar. He loves writing 'odd stories', which are often inspired by his professional experience.

65: SKOT

by Kate Mulvaney

It was Saturday afternoon and me and my friends were at the skate park.

"Let's play copycats," I said.

"Let's play copycats," Jasmine said.

"Let's play copycats," Alicia said.

"Let's play copycats," Charlie said.

"Let's play copycats," Daisy said.

"Let's play copycats," Laura said.

"Start NOW," I said.

"Start NOW," Jasmine said.

"Start NOW," Alicia said.

"Start NOW," Charlie said.

"Start NOW," Daisy said.

"Start NOW," Laura said.

"Game over," I said.

"Game over," all my friends said.

"Stop now," I said.

"OK," said Jasmine, Charlie, Daisy and Laura.

"Stop now," Alicia said.

"Let's skate now," I said.

"Let's skot now," Alicia said.

"Skot?" questioned Laura.

"Wait... skot?" Charlie said.

"Did you mean skate?" I said.

"Yes, I meant skot," Alicia said.

"Repeat after me, skate," I said.

"Skot," replied Alicia.

"Skate," I said.

"Skot," said Alicia.

"Skate."

"Skot."

"Skate."

"Skot."

"SKATE," everyone except Alicia yelled.

"Yeah, that's what I said, skot," said Alicia.

"Gosh," said Daisy.

"Oh, I give up, I'll never be able to say skate," said Alicia sadly.

"Ermmm..." I said. "You just said it."

"Oh my gosh," she said. "Skate, skate, skate, skate."

"Congrats," said Jasmine.

~

Kate Mulvaney's Biography

I'm Kate Mulvaney, I'm in year 7. My hobbies are horse riding, keyboard, Guides, writing, cooking, hanging out with friends and being a big sister. I love animals (including snake/spiders), *Harry Potter* (I'm number one fan) and thriller rides like rollercoasters.

66: AXOLOTLS ARE PEOPLE TOO

by Sam Jeffreys

It was midday and Donald was looking up at the full moon hanging bright and heavy below him.

From behind piped the weedy voice of an axolotl, Roger. "Mr Sweeper, sir? Spare a nibble, sir? Just one, sir? Just one?"

But Donald was not interested – in fact, he took a paracetamol, a long last look at the moon, no notice of Roger, his hat from the ground, and his leave.

Roger, alone with him and himself, stood slouched and mused upon how anything in his world and the others worked the way that they did. It seemed to him that taking comfort in his existence at all was quite enough for one animal all by itself, and therefore bigger things were best left to the Think-Men and the Talk-Men of the land. He'd always wanted to be the first Think-Axolotl, but never could talk his tail round to agreeing. Big decisions always made his toes itch. *Well*, Roger thought, *there's always yesterday*.

~

Sam Jeffreys' Biography

No author biography supplied.

67: STALKING THE NOID

by Mark Johnson

"Listen." The group heard a shrill, jackal-like laugh. Their guide pointed to a bug-eyed furry quadruped in the tree branches. "There's a noid. Look at its eyes." Their Aussie guide clearly enjoyed showing off the more peculiar residents of the outback.

Darting back and forth, its eyes revealed the creature's irrational fear of being watched. "Got to be a mated... there." He pointed to another one, just visible. "Knew it had to be a pair o' noids."

Staring at them, the group was shocked to see one throw something at them. It was one of the creatures' young.

"Irrational when they pair up," their guide said. The little one scampered into the forest. "Don't try to catch him. His parents will smell you and think the little fella's a spy."

A different sound filled the air, a sort of nasal, constricted bark. "Adda noid. That's why these critters are so upset. We'd better move out. Adda noids attack by ripping out your nose."

A larger version of the creature they had watched appeared before them. "Run," screamed their guide, just before he went down in a nosebleed of horror.

~

Mark Johnson's Biography

Mark Johnson is a writer living in Mississippi. He has a

wife, two sons and two cats.
www.markjohnsonauthor.com

68: SKY

by Lilian Indombera Musundi

Her fur was brown, soft and danced in the wind. Her blue eyes made her stand out as unique from the dogs around the village. She followed Sammy everywhere. Today, on their way back from Mama Rosemary, she joined other dogs in chasing eight piglets that were savouring Mama Rosemary's sweet potatoes.

Sky, Simba and Box barked fiercely, biting at the piglets. Seven managed to escape but one unlucky piglet was cornered and in no time only blood was left as evidence of its existence.

Stomachs bulging, the dogs followed Sammy home and slept on the door step. Sky began to groan. Foam came from her mouth, her blue eyes stared fixedly at the sky.

Sammy carried her into the house, placed her in a corner and covered her with his favourite blanket. Sky lay there for three days.

Rumours went around the village: he was mourning a dog. A bad omen, an abomination according to the Ababukusu culture.

On the 4th day he decided to throw Sky in a hole in the neighbour's shamba. The neighbour asked them to pick her up and bury her on their own land. Keep their own barbaric curse.

~

Lilian Indombera Musundi's Biography

Lilian Indombera Musundi is a Kenyan writer, poet, master story teller and performer with a passion for life and expressing it in words. She has published two children's storybooks with Pauline's Publications: *Sheila and Other Stories* and *The Mango Sellers*.

69: LA GROUGHER

by Rebecca Henderson

Wheels skinted across creducial pavement as I faced my mentaxion, the MTA. Mouth gawping wider than a boomnia, a spokuples tongue lolled out before me. With laimpers encircling my hands I incted my cash towards the bellackling hole. Slurping and gurping and blopping ensued, and it was all I could do not to knifier that kraked protty.

Audidling soon turned to quation and I relaxed. Saucerous eyes melded to form a johartonge, and I gasped. Vlover. This could not be.

"Expear, I say." Fists tummeled the MTA. "Give me my tumusk cash."

Comproing. That's all I got in return. The nerve of such an apolatal beast.

My evrophas winkled nearby. Slimmerings filled my mouth as I chuffled into the receptorary. "Mordith Borth speaking."

"Mordith, my pascre, it is over. Pastew. Goodbye."

The twitterings of my wife left me browinhandidah. What was this utter nallus? Over. I rushated into the dead receiver.

The MTA flexceed with refereelasts.

Over.

I priend the masacrassered machine by the very lifine of its easages and throttled it until deremovaties poured from its ears.

"Councts," I hollered, and stuffed my hands within the MTA's loweddler to retrieve my cash.

The MTA lurched. I whudoodled.

A yellahl.

~

Rebecca Henderson's Biography

Rebecca Henderson holds a degree in both German and Creative Writing. She hopes to shift your world perspective through her words, because looking out the same window every day hardly makes for an interesting life.

www.linkedin.com/in/rebecca-henderson

70: CHIPS

by Elwin Estle

"What've ya got, Smitty?"

"The vic is a bag of chips, fell from the top level of the vending machine."

"Accident? Suicide?"

"Looks like it was pushed."

"Suspects?"

"We got a pair of screwy looking perps in custody, but they ain't talkin'. We think they were paid."

~

Elwin Estle's Biography

No author biography supplied.

71: WHISKEY IN THE JAR

by Filippo Contalbi

Dig. Dig. Dig. More digging.

My shovel cut the mud and my foot gave the final push. Jebby the Jedediah was sitting on the cart licking his elbows, and Porter the Mailman crouched on the edge of the ditch to look at my work.

And of course, my trusty jar of whiskey was tied to my belt.

"Where are we going?" asked the jar.

"We're going to China," I said.

"Oh," it replied. "And where is China?"

"Well, it's down below," I said. "Mr Henry said one can dig to China, if willing. Good man, that Mr Henry."

"How will we know we'll be in China and not somewhere else when we arrive?"

I stuck the spade in the ground and scratched my chin. That was a good question. I knew that was a clever jar. My ma warned me not to talk to chatty jars, especially drunk ones. She said they put evil thoughts in your head, but that one seemed alright. Very nice fellow. "I guess we'll know when we're there. I may be no educated city boy, but I know my digging."

"Of course you do," said the jar.

~

Filippo Contalbi's Biography

Born in Verona, Italy on the 31st of August 1997. Studied in British schools in Milan (Bilingual European

School and St Louis School). Currently studies BA English and Creative Writing Joint Honours at Brunel University London.

72: CAMPIP SECRETS

by Louise Burgess

"Such riffraff," screamed Loxy, while scoffing another campip up her second blowhole, the one closer to her red glittered wings rather than the one on her head.

"The body of mind tells the tale of towers," replied Adalia in a calmer tone, while carefully tossing a campip into her own blowhole, the purple type of course.

This remark caused Loxy to flutter her red wings in anger while whispering, "A cranky old lady would die for a grapefruit."

Suddenly, the pretty Wickall that Loxy had been resting on was engulfed in purple flames, causing the petal with campips to fall out of sight.

This meant only one thing of course. Faerydae had heard the passionate conversation between the two fairies.

Loxy and Adalia both knew they would suffer the Stormfawn as punishment for discussing such secrets.

~

Louise Burgess's Biography

Written by Louise Burgess in dedication to her heart warrior son Emmet.

www.loopybwritingpage.wordpress.com

73: THAT STOLEN FIGURINE TELLS THE TALE OF TOWERS

by Len Saculla

He's full of it. Even though most of his experience on his travels was within the dark pocket and then slightly mildewed bag of the thief. Of course, returned, that figurine – let's call him Sparky because he sheds only a little light on our existence – is the toast of the campus and the news media.

But once it gets quiet, I call out to him, "Hey, short stature, why have you got so much to say for yourself?"

"What? Who are you with that deep, stony voice?"

"I'm Henry the reclining sculpture. I've been here way longer than you have and command some respect. My master was a Nobel artist."

"Nobles will die come the porcelain revolution, big guy. In the meantime, people are celebrating me because I achieved movement."

"Only by another's hand. I am forever posed mid-movement. Is that not graceful?"

"What should I be grateful for, you big lump?"

"My intellect, my friendship. My eyes that tell me that the guy who stole you is still at large. He's not quite my size but he's large enough to pick you up and take you far away from these university towers, their dreaming spires."

"You're just jeal–"

~

Len Saculla's Biography

Len Saculla has been published in magazines and on websites including *Wordland* and *Tube Flash*, as well as in several anthologies from American publisher Kind of a Hurricane Press. He had a flash fiction nominated for a Pushcart Prize in 2015.

74: DAMNATION & TEA

by Craig Douglas

As dusk fell, I endeavoured to atone for my sins of which there was a rotten plentitude and, in order to escape Hell, I was ordered to drink seven gallons of water from a holy well.

"I have lived a life of purity," I claimed.

"Sinner," shouted He.

"But Father Withers, why are you sitting in a tree?"

"I sit here for your sins in splintered agony."

"I did not sin," I sniggered, as I sipped the holy water.

"Codswallop. Thou have sinned therefore thou art a sinner. And lo, the holy water burns your throat. Thou art condemned to the fiery pits below."

The sun began to rise. The night had disintegrated into day, with not a sign of Hell, damnation or doomsday.

He slumbered in his tree and unfortunately fell, then consequently cracked his skull upon the well and mystically metamorphosed to stone. Meanwhile, I frolicked in the lilac light of dawn when I discovered the holy water was steaming tea and truly not holy at all.

I still visit Father Withers at the holy well. The fellow never seems to age, and he never accepts a cup of tea, which to me seems rather strange.

~

Craig Douglas's Biography

Craig-Douglas Whipp is a writer of absurd, existential stories that delve into the unfathomable depths of the abyss. He is also a qualified photographer specialised in capturing otherworldly visions of the natural world.

75: FISH TALES AND CARGO PLANES

by Laura-Liisa Klaas

There's not much to do in this adorable log cabin in the middle of a meadow surrounded by gargantuan (but in a nice whimsical way) apple trees.

Therefore, entertainment must be sought elsewhere. And that is why we meet Maria in the middle of a nearby field, trying to desperately hitch a flight off EasyJet cargo planes flying above.

No such luck — it's Wednesday. And Wednesday is when cargo planes are forbidden to land in the field where Maria is waiting.

Maria doesn't know this because she is yet to learn to read and would therefore not have known to look at the poster SO CLEARLY visible on a nearby tree. Silly Maria.

So after seven hours of waiting (she is resilient, let's give her that) Maria returns, somewhat sombre, to the dull but cute log cabin and resumes what she was doing before she got this great idea (being sarcastic here). She picks up her knitting and starts to work on it. After all, the mermaid tail blanket must be finished before she turns 70 — and that's next month.

She hopes that Jorma will come back from Azerbaijan for the celebrations. He's been gone for 15 years already.

~

Laura-Liisa Klaas's Biography

I'm a 30-something Estonian girl living and working in Aberdeen, Scotland and loving it. This year I made myself a promise to start writing my book and therefore I am trying my hand first with the awesome challenges here.

www.schmunny.wordpress.com

76: ONCE

by Glyn Roberts

Once upon a time, in a land far away, in a beautiful palace, lived a handsome cliché.

Two travellers, man and wife, sought the cliché.

"Look yonder, 'pon palace walls. Is that a damsel distress-wise I peruse perchance?" asked the husband.

"Why speak like that?" demanded his wife. "You were born in Salford, not the middle ages."

They sauntered up to the palace walls and watched warily as one of the mutant zombie, vampire defenders ominously cranked the handle of a Gatling gun.

"How are we going to get out of this?" she wondered. Then turning to an imaginary camera, "And where is this absurd story going?"

Her husband squinted at the sky where a spectral finger pointed to beyond the horizon. "Thank heaven, a deus ex machine."

She looked at him quizzically, as did some dear readers following this passage.

"A deus ex machine," he repeated. "A plot device whereby a seemingly unsolvable problem is resolved by the unexpected intervention of some new event."

"Oh, that deus ex machine," nodded his wife. "A writer's device to get out of literary jail. Good, now we can wake up, and none of this nonsense ever happened, even once upon a time."

~

Glyn Roberts' Biography

Glyn Roberts is a professional writer and performance poet. He leads writing workshops and runs the monthly poetry evening at Pontardawe Arts Centre.

Member and current Treasurer of Neath Writers' Group, he has produced three poetry collections.

www.sites.google.com/site/poetglyn/poetglyn

77: CASANOVA

by Betty Hattersley

William Wormsearth had always been different from other worms, although, exceeding in literary talents, he'd always been down to earth.

He originated from the Lumbricidae family. A family quite respected in some parts of the garden.

However, William didn't have much luck wooing the ladies with his literary prose.

Once again William had fallen in love with a beautiful red-headed lady worm. Her name was Rubellus.

William spent hours trying to compost the perfect verse for his true love. Hours and hours he spent searching for the right words to turn her head. Perhaps he would present it to her with a bouquet of dead leaves.

Then one morning he saw her entwined with another under the fruit tree.

William was devastated, hurt, an emotional mess. But before he got too much of an emotional mess, out the corner of his eye, he saw the most gorgeous, voluptuous worm he'd ever seen, slowly squiggling along the path.

His mind, just for a moment, turned to Rubellus – then with a shrug and a smile William thought to himself, *sod it*, and made his way to pursue a new romance.

~

Betty Hattersley's Biography

I've been writing for many years and have had numerous poems and short stories published in anthologies, newspapers, calendars and magazines.

I've written a small book (yet to be published) about the funny side of my outside catering days.

78: ROCKY

by Alan Barker

Rocky looked like a normal teenager, but his eating habits were not.

He loved chips, not from the chip shop, but chips of rock bought specially by his dad from the local quarry.

Each day he would have sand and cement porridge for breakfast, pea gravel and chips for dinner and sticky rocky tarmac pudding for tea.

During the school holidays he would dive into a local stream and eat pebbles until he was so full he could not surface. When the water level went down he would climb out for his next meal.

One day, there was a tremendous storm and he was swept into the Thames. London. Wow. He didn't know where to look. Stone everywhere.

Should he nibble St Paul's or begin at Tower Bridge? Yes, Tower Bridge. Alarm was raised as one of the towers began to sink, so Rocky rushed off to St. Paul's.

He was really enjoying the dome – marble was a specialist taste – but was arrested for 'eating with intent'.

He appeared in court and was sentenced to six months in prison.

He loved the idea and asked for a longer sentence. The prison was built of... stone.

~

Alan Barker's Biography

A retired English/Drama teacher, I live in South Wales.

Writing plays and short stories is my passion, although I enjoy turning personal experiences into poetry, e.g. urology doctors and nurses, coffee bar waitresses, dental receptionists and soldiers.

79: THE WISDOM OF A CHILD

by Phil Woodford

The wait to board the aircraft was long. An announcement was made. "Passengers for Speedy Boarding please come forward."

A grunt from our eight year old Granddaughter who exclaimed in decibels that rang around the holding pen, "Speedy boarding. Do you mean people actually PAY for Speedy boarding? Why, Grandma?"

"Well, some people like to board the aircraft first."

"Are they disabled, Grandma?"

"No, people with disabilities are boarded first."

"Then why do people actually PAY to get on first? Why are we late leaving, Grandma?"

"Well, the lady said it was technical problems on the inbound aircraft which facilitated its late arrival."

"Perhaps a bit fell off, Grandma?"

"No, dear, bits don't fall off."

"Grandma, I'm not boarding if bits fall off."

"Don't be silly, it's all perfectly safe."

"Then why has that man over there got a green face?"

"It's just the lighting in here, the man will turn pink when he gets outside."

"Does that mean if we crash he won't know how to put on his lifejacket?"

"I don't know, read your book, we're taking off in a minute."

"Grandma, that man's face didn't go pink. It's still GREEN."

~

Phil Woodford's Biography

No author biography supplied.

80: EXCERPT FROM THE UNWRITTEN DIARY OF EDUARD GERT OTTO: ALSERGRUND, VIENNA, 1913

by Amanda Garzia

"My Id is flaring up. As is my Superego," I complained, arching my back.

"Call them in."

The professor handed us a sheet as we sat on the couch.

'Chew over this pickle and draw a conclusion', it read.

"What?" I objected.

"You've booked an examination have you not? This is it."

"Jentacular gherkin. Glaucous, fulvous, lusty-gallant, incarnadine," burbled Id, attempting the task with gusto, one hand in a pickle jar, the other in paint.

"What are you doing, Gadarene swine?" Superego thundered.

"Chewing and drawing."

Their antics made me squirm but I understood, applauding the professor's madness explorandi. He had set us this task in order to observe their reaction. I thus sat back while they manifested their lunacy.

"Repent Bohemian freak," lashed out Superego. "The pickle is evil, heaven or hell the conclusion."

"Mind your own business, holier-than-thou Bapdismal John."

They bickered splenetically. They were going to fail. Undoubtedly.

"Time up," the professor declared, taking me aside.

"They," he said, "lived up to their roles splendidly. You, on the contrary, did nothing whatsoever to mediate, failing abysmally."

"They send shivers down my spine and *I* disappoint?"

"Inveterate invertebrate. The problem is your spine," he concluded. "You have none."

~

Amanda Garzia's Biography

Amanda Garzia was born in Canada and moved to Malta as a child. Now that her son is too old for bedtime stories, she's busy writing the story of her first years on the island and contributing to English-language publications.

Find Amanda on Twitter: @amanda_garzia

81: FROM A VOICE RECORDER

by Tulip Chowdhury

Patient: Why is God referred to as 'He'? I have a problem with male domination. Not marrying a man or 'He'.

Therapist: One doesn't have to get married, you can have a partner.

Patient: I'm a church goer and Mama says I have to marry a man soon or I'll end up a spinster. Why is God a 'He' in holy books?

Therapist: Women were at home more when religious books were written. Maybe if a new religion develops then God will be a woman. Many great people were men, like Einstein, Archimedes, Plato...

Patient: There you go. But you came from a woman?

Therapist: Yes. But women can't make babies alone.

Patient: I'm sure they will from the day God starts being a 'She'. The energy will shift truly to female power.

Therapist: Who knows, miracles can happen.

Patient: Perhaps religious books will be revised and God will be a 'She'.

Therapist: We can talk more about that in your next session.

Patient: I want to come tomorrow, making God a 'She' will take time.

~

Tulip Chowdhury's Biography

Tulip Chowdhury resides in Massachusetts, USA. Other books from her are *Red, Blue, Purple*, *Stars in the Sky*, *Reaching Beyond Words*, *Rain Drops*, *Nature and Love* and non-fiction *April*, co-authored with Andrew Eagle, an Australian born writer.

82: PLAYMATES

by Judith Wolfgang

What is silly to one is not necessarily silly to another. But I always love a challenge.

Her name was Samantha and she was my imaginary playmate. It was a great relationship. She always shared and let me have my way, most of the time.

The hard part was remembering other people could not see Samantha, so I had to be careful when other people came my way. If I did not, it looked like I was talking to myself.

Sam and I had a lot of fun having hide-and-seek picnics, playing dolls and dress-up.

I still miss her, but as we grow older, do we really need imaginary playmates?

~

Judith Wolfgang's Biography

Judith Helen Wolfgang likes to write. Whether it is the most recent poem contest or the latest challenge, writing is part of who she is. To use words to express your deepest thoughts, is a challenge in itself.

83: THE HUCKLING STICK

by David Turnbull

The huckling stick had been cutsied too long. It was all out of valance and hefling at odd tragedies. Harnaby couldn't meyster a fleng from it. He kept huckling the onlobber by mistake.

"Who the dell cutsied this huckling?" he cried, as another onlobber was harried away, head all rupped in spinnaker and trown draper. "It's all long on its tipsy and short at the bottly bit."

All the stick makers snuffled their feegs and turned their peepers downways.

Another onlooker steffed up to the murk, nobbles knocking – face as pale as a gust.

Harnaby whocked the stick at the tweezle.

Hangang.

The onlooker got huckled. Down he went, like a twee in a forage. The tweezle dunced a jug and stuck out its vorty lung. Seeing this, Harnaby threw a wobbly. It hit the tweezle on the twonk. Pop went the tweezle and turned into a zoog.

"You can't huck a tweezle with a wobbly," complained the referender.

"You can if your huckling stick is long on its tipsy," insisted Harnaby and twanged the referender on the kosser.

Great hubilation.

The onlobbers harooed and hefted Harnaby by his hat string.

~

David Turnbull's Biography

David Turnbull is a Scotsman who lives in London. He is a member of the Clockhouse London group of genre writers. Most recently in *Ghost Highways* by Midnight Street Press and *Forever Vacancy Colours in Darkness*.

www.tumsh.co.uk

84: TROUBLED WATERS

by Mark Lewis

A river a thousand paces wide is a storyteller without equal; she never tells her stories to a living soul. So many adventures in her history: dramatic river crossings on flimsy rafts, Viking raiders, the start of voyages to the Nine Seas.

The river is wild, having never been bridged. In her dreams, a bridge made of the drowned spans across her. Thankfully, there are no plans by worldly hands to build such a grisly crossing and the dead remain sunk, or at least those parts left by the hungry fish.

The river could tell so many tales. There was Old Tom Lacey the fisherman, whose line was caught by the King of the Hungry Fish, dragging him in. Then there was the maiden, Clara, who visited the river with her fiancé but walked home alone. The fiancé was never found.

Most recently, there was the poet, who, admiring the rays of the sun breaking through pendulous clouds, did not watch his step and did not see the tentacle that wrapped itself around his leg. A river a thousand paces wide is a storyteller without equal but she keeps her own secrets.

~

Mark Lewis's Biography

M M Lewis is widely published in the independent press, including the *British Fantasy Society Journal*, *Theaker's Quarterly* and *Wordland*. He enjoys having a license to write nonsense and more of his work can be found here:

www.syntheticscribe.wordpress.com

85: THE LEGEND OF THE RAVEN'S ROAR IS GOOD FOR YOU

by Ian Steadman

The Doctor smiles from behind his pigskin desk.

"These are the words," he says, sickeningly grey. "Eat them, eat them whole."

You look at the jar. 'Black', it says. 'Murder'. 'Treacherous'. 'Cawfulious'. 'Ravenish'.

"What is this?" you ask, the words sticking on the tip of your tongue.

The Doctor says nothing. His nose is too sharp, his brow too feathered. When he eats a biscuit he nibbles it like your grandmother.

"I can't eat these. What are they written on, anyway? They look like bones."

"No," he laughs. "No. Bones? Not at all. Those are teeth."

You unscrew the cap and pull one out. It seems to be an incisor. On the curved side is etched the word 'Blarkry'.

"Do I swallow it?"

His head bobs.

"Do you have any water?"

"No."

It feels strange in your mouth at first, an ivory pebble, cold and precise. When you swallow it, you can't hold back a sneeze.

The Doctor smiles, flaps his arrings. Turning his raveman head to the sky, he shrilly caws his meak.

~

Ian Steadman's Biography

Ian Steadman is a writer from the south of England. His stories have recently been published by Black Static and Unsung Stories, although his work has appeared in numerous zines and websites over the years.

Find Ian on Twitter: @steadmanfiction

86: TUESDAY AFTERNOONS

by Sandra Unerman

Significant understanding rains heavily every Tuesday afternoon. On Wednesdays, the evaporation thickens into small mists over the knitting needles and turns the socks into clouds of pineapples. On Thursdays, significant understanding jumps both ways in and out of the clouds and unravels the pineapples into strands of liquorice. You can see them melting over the trees. The blackbirds get stuck and the crows complain horribly.

Fridays, everyone stays indoors, so understanding pales into insignificance and weeps quietly into the doormat. But on moonlit nights, the mice eat the liquorice and sing songs too beautiful to remember. The significant rain runs down the hills and the raindrops turn blue. That's when the elephants come out, not too close to the mice, to breathe in the understanding and tramp back up into the hills, where they wait for the rains to begin again.

~

Sandra Unerman's Biography

Sandra Unerman is a writer of fantasy and a member of the London Clockhouse Writers' Group. Her novel, *Spellhaven*, is due out from Mirror World Publishing in August 2017. For details of her short stories, see her blog:

www.sandraunermanwriter.com

87: GRUMPY SHEEP –VS– THE WORLD

by Jonathan Macho

It was a sunny day, quite unlike most in the hills and valleys of Wales, and Grumpy Sheep stood in his field and chewed the cud. After a while, he looked to the left. After a while longer, he looked to the right. His vigil complete, he let out a sigh.

This was his life.

"OY."

Grumpy Sheep started. He was very much alone at that moment and, after his expert glances in both available directions, he was certain nobody was there to OY him.

"IT'S ME," the voice continued. "THE WORLD."

Right. That explained that then.

"WHY ARE YOU SO GRUMPY, GRUMPY SHEEP?" the World demanded in a surprisingly strong Welsh accent. "YOU'VE GOT THE CUD. YOU'VE GOT THE SUN. I'M DOING MY BEST HERE, MATE."

In response, Grumpy Sheep let out another sigh.

"THAT'S WHAT I'M TALKING ABOUT." The World was despairing.

Grumpy Sheep was about to say welcome to my world, but wasn't sure how that could apply when talking to THE World, and so chewed some more cud instead.

"PLEASE, MUN. JUST ANSWER ME."

"What's my name again?" Grumpy Sheep asked, looking warily up into the pretty blue sky.

"WHY, GRUMPY SHEEP."

"That answer your question?"

~

Jonathan Macho's Biography

Jonathan Macho is a recently-ish graduated student, lost in the big wide world, with a passion for writing and a frenzied imagination. He lives in Cardiff with his family and a talking space raccoon who definitely exists.

88: THE CASE OF THE CULTURAL ATTACHÉ

by Morag Watson

The whimsical mermaid was left flailing on the rocks, in the glass tumbler alongside the whiskey.

"Dram drim drumkit," she inhaled meagrely.

Tranquility came, requesting a reprieve from the Ning Nang Nong's bongos. Spike acquiesced, but went back on his word. And the word was renege. Grease was also the word, but not the term used in this Case of the Cultural Attaché. The Attaché yelled a blanket of peace and calm over the latter sentence, such that Crow's inky scowl was ever-present in the blink.

Trickery had lost all respect for the percussion section, bongos included, and its ethical stance on nothingness.

Consequently, using the intense, diluted nothingness of concentrated distillation, he mocked all humanity with dry understanding. All humanity and kettle drums, that is. For kettle drums, and their intrinsic lack of essence, bring nothing but a crowd of isolation; isolation offering little other than the tantalising possibility of meretricious trickery.

Crow's ever-present scowl remained non-existent, allowing the Cultural Attaché to solve clues — unhindered by those clichés glued to a percussive concerto of fell running. And so it was that the nefarious whiskey exposed both the mermaid and her esoteric paradiddles.

~

Morag Watson's Biography

No author biography supplied.

89: IT'S A BREEZE

by Carol Moeke

"Chair, Number Eleven, is like a summer breeze. Take it if you like. Put it where you like and let the breeze take you if you like. It's already wafting your way, wafting you away, so hold on tight, Number Eleven.

"Number Eight, your time is up. It's time to come down. Lower the umbrella. Lean to the right. No, to the right, that's right. You were right all the time. And right on time. Collect your deposit as you leave."

The leaves catch the breeze and look for the chair. The chair is in the air being wafted. The leaves join the fun and flutter. And the sneeze of the breeze throws us all off course, of course.

Number Twelve saves the day and chimes in with a warning to ring the changes. "Go with the flow," Twelve bellows to those below. Those above think it's all a breeze, except for Number Eleven. He knows it's a chair.

A chair in the air makes you aware of all that life blows at you.

~

Carol Moeke's Biography

No author biography supplied.

90: THE LIGHT AT THE END OF THE TUNNEL IS NOT ENOUGH

by Ejder S. Raif

Frederick was about to explode like a nuclear bomb. His treasure hunt was in shambles. All his friends had disappeared into thin air. He was left stranded in the forest like a lost lemon, surrounded by trees overhead like a tunnel. He kept expecting a train to arrive through this tunnel, but he remembered that he wasn't on a train track.

He spotted two crazy birds fighting childishly over food.

"Where's a referee when you need them?" asked Frederick.

He persisted with the treasure hunt alone, but he found nothing. In frustration, he yelled into the great open space, sounding like an angry lion scaring off a pack of hyenas, terrifying all living things who fled like a bullet from a shotgun. If he had yelled inside a building, all the windows would smash.

"Hey," called a familiar voice.

Frederick spun around, nearly falling over, expecting to see a stack of hay. He saw Robin, not Batman's partner, or the actual bird, but his friend.

Frederick was unhappy that the treasure hunt had failed. He left the forest with Robin, his face doleful like he was about to burst into tears, flooding the entire forest, creating a deep blue ocean.

~

Ejder S. Raif's Biography

Ejder S. Raif has been published in Issue 2 of *Boscombe Revolution* and in NUHA Foundation's 2013 *Blogging Prizes*. He lives in London and works as a Support Worker, as well as an Assistant Communications Officer.

91: CANDY

by Martin Russo

Colourful clay is omnipresent, much like candy.

Yes, but if only I could eat clay like I used to eat candy then my life would be a lot simpler. I am, as they might say, slightly keen on pottery and the thought of a big dollop of clay in my hand to squeeze, mould, punch and knock into something semi decent, fills my heart with joy.

I was fascinated with clay from a young age. It started when I used to shuffle it into my mouth when a teacher swiftly suggested pottery to my mother at the school gates.

It never left me, the joy of clay. Like candy, I could never quite get enough. Now, I have built a multi-coloured clay house. I knocked up my kitchen in clay, made shoes, belts and speakers.

I see clay everywhere. I mainly use reds, yellows and greens. My yellow clay elephant completed my clay zoo in my garden. I dedicated it to my then lover, Veronica Piles, but it did not work, as she left.

And whenever I am introduced to someone at a dinner party, I normally say, "Hi, I love clay, how about you?"

~

Martin Russo's Biography

Martin Russo mainly writes poetry, plays, flash and literary fiction.

92: A BEAUTIFUL MIND

by Sueleen Swann

I queue in the line marked 'WOMAN'. I count the number of souls ahead and estimate my wait will be an hour.

The whispered message slowly passes down the line.

"Beauty or brain," the soul in front of me relays. "You are only allowed to choose one."

Beauty or brain? In my last body, I was beautiful but dumb.

By the time I reach the podium, I am still undecided.

"Hello, God. I would like both please," I whisper.

"Impossible. The rule is that you choose ONE for your next life," he replies.

"But why? I don't want to be dumb and ugly. I want both in equal measures."

He scowls at me and roars, "Enough. I am tired." A long pause. He consults the *Book of Life* and looks at me. "Very well then, you may have both."

There is a bright light and I open my eyes to see my new parents peering over me.

"We shall name him John Forbes Nash Jnr," I hear my mother say.

Not quite what I wanted. But at least I have a beautiful mind.

~

Sueleen Swann's Biography

BKA Fay, I was born and raised in Fiji but moved to the

UK over 15 years ago.

I am a newbie to writing, currently 'in between jobs' and love my family, friends and food.

93: A PINEAPPLE MOMENT

by Graham Curtis

"A late night shoots pineapple with a machine gun," it says.

"What?" I say.

The machine says, "A light knight shouts 'pina colada' with a spitting gun."

"You're mad," I say.

Again it says, "Light-weight shorts pee in a spittoon gun."

"What is this gun?" I say.

"Nonsense starts with 'green ideas sleep furiously' and ends with the spittoon gun," the machine spits out.

"Nonsense," I say. "Don't quote Chomsky at me. Green ideas can sleep furiously. You can have black thoughts, so you can have green ideas. You can sleep fitfully or quietly, so you can sleep furiously. And thoughts can be unconscious or asleep."

"But the gun," it cries out as only machines can, "and the spittoon. What of the gun and the spittoon?"

"The spittoon is the target for the mouth," I offer, "the gun of abuse, spitting out its nonsense."

"So my black thoughts, quietly unconscious, are trying to leave through directed speech which turns out to be nonsense," the machine says.

"That's it," I reply.

"I'm cured," the machine exaltedly claims, as only a therapised machine can.

"That's right," I say and switch it off.

~

Graham Curtis's Biography

Graham Curtis has published a number of short stories and pieces of flash fiction over the years. Having worked in the university sector for over three decades, he now enjoys himself through writing, painting and travelling often and widely.

94: WHERE THERE'S SMOKE

by C.I. Selkirk

"Pinocchio asked you a question?"

"Run, run, as fast as you can. You can't catch me..."

"Yeah, yeah, I know who you are. What did he ask you? Do you think he knows?"

"Pat-a-cake, pat-a-cake."

"Oh no. What did you say?"

"Rub-a-dub-dub."

"Good save. So, is everything ready?"

"The sky is falling. The sky is falling."

"Not again. You've had weeks. What's gone wrong?"

"Hey diddle diddle."

"You're kidding. It's always a drama with those two. I don't know why they don't just call it a day. Are they still coming?"

"I'll huff and I'll puff."

"All right, calm down. No need to get violent. Just have a quiet word with them. Tell them to behave for Pinocchio's sake. It's not every day a hunk of wood comes to life."

"Hickory dickory dock."

"Blimey, you're right. We'd better get going or we'll be late."

"All the king's horses and all the king's men."

"Exactly. Let's get this surprise party started."

"Party? Is someone having a party?"

"Pinocchio, hi. I thought you were inside."

"Just stepped out for a ciggie."

"Three blind mice. Carving knife."

"He's right. Pinocchio, you're on fire."

"That's all, folks. The end."

~

C.I. Selkirk's Biography

No author biography supplied.

95: WHISKEY

by Mangal Patel

Whiskey on the table jumps both ways as the billionaires watch in disbelief.

"I suppose anything is possible in space."

Dick's sanguine remark annoys his fellow traveller, William.

"How can you be so calm when we are hurtling towards the moon in this tin can you call *The Ultimate Tourist*?" William demands.

"I've faced death many times on Earth, including the time I fell out of a hot air balloon. This journey is nothing to having your life flash before your eyes."

Dick's languid manner grates on William's already frazzled nerves.

"This silence would die for a grapefruit." William hopes this obtuse comment will evoke some interest from his laid-back companion.

Dick merely begins snoring.

It's no use, the two entrepreneurial billionaires are hopelessly incompatible. Dick is in search of the ultimate thrill whilst William is in search of the elusive star that rains heavily.

What relief all that wetness would give to the parched Earth. What thirst it would quench, the philanthropic nerdy billionaire muses.

"But there's not even a drop of whiskey in sight," William complains bitterly to their pilot, Whiskey the chimpanzee, who jumps both ways frenetically navigating the first two tourists to the Moon.

~

Mangal Patel's Biography

Mangal, a recent entrant to the wonderful world of writing, has a number of short stories published on the web and in hardback anthologies. She is a retired IT Director, is married and has twins. Lives in London UK.

96: DIE FLEDERMAUS

by Nick Black

The memo from my boss read 'GET A JELLY DIE FLEDERMAUS TO SALLY'S PARTY – ON TIME'. I looked on the back of the note for any indication of flavour, colour, conductor, turned it over and over but there was nothing. I was already on probation after I'd been caught walking around my boss's office in her high heels while she was having her afternoon nap – I hadn't expected the clacking to wake her.

You'd be surprised how hard it is to render German opera in gelatine. The high notes never set. The wobble... The wobble... I couldn't take my eyes off the wobble, screaming at me from the front basket as I cycled my plated effort through the midtown traffic, half praying a truck would jump the lights and smear me across the tarmac. Was Sally the six year old, the eight year old or the 32 year old daughter? Did she have any food allergies? Pineapple chunks slid down the quivering sides of the opera, a transparent red mountain in musical meltdown.

If only I'd had the talents to find another job, one where I could afford to buy my own high heels.

~

Nick Black's Biography

Nick Black's stories have been published by literary magazines including *(b)OINK zine, The Lonely Crowd, Spelk Fiction, Open Pen, Severine, Funhouse, Firefly,*

Razur Cuts and *Litro*, with more coming soon to *Jellyfish Review* and *The Ham*.

www.fuzzynick.wordpress.com

97: HERE COMES THE BRIDE

by Alva Holland

Something old, something new, something borrowed, something blue, Celeste mused.

"GN-z11 – that'll do for the old thing – tick.

"A refulgent diamond star discovered in 2014 – new enough – tick.

"Roscosmos won't miss that miniscule space station it thought would change the world – tick. Don't worry, Vlad, I'll return it.

"One gem of cyan nebula – pocketed – tick.

"The dress – a Milky Way streak of lace and effervescent bubbles. Orion will go supernova. We'll hit Deep Space Nine together. Staggering.

"Getting side-tracked. Ice grains turning to sugar molecules – cake decorations – tick.

"Bridesmaids. Canis, Ursa and Draco. Triple special effect lighting.

"Guest list – God (no, not you – too much of a distraction). Universal participation – if you can get here, you're invited. Orion will be impressed.

"Orion – hmmm. Where the hell is the little star-gazer? Him and his precious celestial equator. Things will change when we're married. For a start, those protostar groupies will go. Shallow flickering cosmic dust, no substance.

"Honeymoon? Andromeda. Stellar nightlife.

"Nearly done. Da, have I asked you to do the aisle spacewalk with me? Yes, I'll always be your baby. I know – separation is difficult. Look out for me – Orion's bride, forever in your shadow."

~

Alva Holland's Biography

Alva Holland is an Irish writer from Dublin, first published by *Ireland's Own Winning Writers Annual* in 2015.

Twice a winner of Ad Hoc Fiction's weekly flash competition, she's also featured in *The People's Friend* and *Firefly Magazine*.

Find Alva on Twitter: @Alva1206

98: ANTHONY BURNED A HOLE IN THE RAIN

by Christopher Iacono

Anthony burned a hole in the rain. His mother had told him to come home before the rain, but here he was, under the clouds wringing themselves out over the grassy marshlands fenced in by shimmering reeds. He delighted in the flames slowly nibbling away at his arm, leaving behind charred bits of flesh that clung to his blackened bones.

Then someone called him. "Excuse me, young man," said a man in a black robe standing in front of the reeds. "Can you lead me to the pond?"

"But, sir, it's right behind you."

"Oh, yes, you're right." The man grabbed the front of Anthony's shirt and threw him through the reeds. His body splashed into the green water.

Once he recovered, he drifted along the surface of the pond, while the crackling fire was eating its way toward his elbow. He sighed. At least he could still sing.

"Sheep may safely graze on pasture, when the shepherd guards them well..."

He nearly choked on the rain entering his mouth, but that didn't stop him from finishing his song.

~

Christopher Iacono's Biography

Christopher Iacono lives with his wife and son in Massachusetts. You can learn more about him on his website.

www.cuckoobirds.org

99: FALLEN

by Peter Jordan

The man felt the pain of growth. It was a pain he had felt before. His skin was splitting, but he didn't want to cry out. He got up and put on his dressing gown and shuffled to the exercise yard, shoulders slumped forward, head down. He waited and, when the moment was right, he let his dressing gown fall to the concrete. His beautiful white wings were released. He flapped them so hard they cracked like whips. The orderlies just stood and stared. At first he didn't move, then slowly, he lifted. Unsteady at first, he lifted up and over the concrete walls and razor wire.

Dr Gallo, the senior psychiatrist, looked out of his office window and saw the man fly upwards in a slow circle, towards a break in the clouds. For a full five minutes he watched him rising higher and higher into the sky. It was only when he was no more than a dot in the heavens that Dr Gallo fell to his knees and prayed.

~

Peter Jordan's Biography

Peter Jordan is this year's winner of the Bare Fiction Flash prize. His work has appeared in numerous literary magazines. In addition, seven of his stories are in anthologies. His short story collection, *Untouchable*, will be published this summer.

Find Peter on Twitter: @pm_jordan

100: A FUNNY THING HAPPENED TO ME ON THE WAY TO THE PARTICLE ACCELERATOR

by Helen Rye

I see from your resume that you are something of an expert in superparticleisation. This is obviously an area we value highly, here at the Large Hairdo Collider.

We are in the process, as you know, of accelerating a collection of old-school footballers with mullets very quickly into isotopic 1980s New Romantics, in the hope of discovering the elusive Mod particle, which Science believes to be responsible for the cosmic impulse towards the neat but angular bob. If the experiment is successful, it is hoped we may also observe spontaneously created Sta-Prest. We have already unexpectedly isolated a new form of atonic orchestral punk-thrash, which nobody could have predicted (although some say it was there in the equations). What a time to be alive.

But let me show you to your microscope and volumising spray, Professor – just past the accidental black hole containment station (in case of singularity creation, please break glass), but do mind your step.

Oh. That was unfortunate. Well, very best of luck with whatever dimension that eventually spits you out into, Professor, and I'll get HR to fire in a note containing your contract and a severance package suitable to your unimaginable new form.

~

Helen Rye's Biography

Helen Rye lives in Norwich and writes fiction on her phone while burning pasta. She has won the Bath Flash Fiction Award, been shortlisted for the Bridport Flash Fiction Prize and is a Best Small Fictions 2017 nominee. 80% biscuits.

Find Helen on Twitter: @helenrye

A FINAL NOTE

Lesley and I would like to say one last THANK YOU to all the authors featured in this anthology. Their generosity is helping support a very worthy charity and it's an honour to present their stories in this collection.

Don't forget to check my website for more writing challenges – there will be many more appearing in the future. You will be able to find all the details here: www.christopherfielden.com/writing-challenges/

I will say farewell Bristol-style:

Cheers me dears,

Chris Fielden

Printed in Great Britain
by Amazon